"Bedroom. Now."

Logan stopped at the bed, pulled down his shirt only to unbutton it in record time, and swiftly yanked down the covers.

God bless America, he was built like...like the men in her dreams. They all had his kind of body—muscled, a subtle six-pack, just enough hair that she could play with it during the cooldown after and a trim waist that led to a very impressive package.

"This is the part where you take off your shorts," Kensey teased. "Unless you'd like me to—"

They hit the floor before he could finish.

He smiled. The kind of smile that changed his face. Made him look sexy as all get-out. Then he pulled her onto his lap for a kiss.

She kissed him back. Deep and real and just messy enough to match the urgency that was coiling inside him like a rattler.

"You're gorgeous," he said as he tumbled her onto the bed.

Dear Reader,

Welcome back to my Three Wicked Nights miniseries!

You may remember Logan McCabe from *Intrigue Me*. He was the heroine's hunky brother, a former special ops soldier, a man who'd gone above and beyond before returning home to face yet another battle—adjusting to civilian life. He tackles the problem head-on, starting a security firm that employs vets, like himself, who want to make a difference.

In *One Sizzling Night*, Logan has gone to Boston for a security conference and has been invited to test out his college friend's amazing "smart" apartment. To Logan's surprise, he won't be spending the week alone. There's a woman in residence, Kensey Roberts, and you won't believe what she's wearing when he meets her!

They not only spend some sizzling nights together, but when Logan finally unravels the mystery of Kensey, it puts them both in the line of fire!

I hope you're enjoying this series. Look for the third Three Wicked Nights book coming in September.

You can always reach me at joleigh@joleigh.com or jomk.tumblr.com. I love hearing from readers!

All my best wishes,

Jo Leigh

Jo Leigh

One Sizzling Night

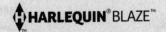

Recycling programs
for this product may
not exist in your area.

ISBN-13: 978-0-373-79884-1

One Sizzling Night

Copyright © 2016 by Jolie Kramer

Printed in U.S.A.

www.Harlequin.com

Jo Leigh is from Los Angeles and always thought she'd end up living in Manhattan. So how did she end up in Utah in a tiny town with a terrible internet connection, being bossed around by a houseful of rescued cats and dogs? What the heck, she says, predictability is boring. Jo has written more than forty-five novels for Harlequin. Visit her website at joleigh.com or contact her at joleigh@joleigh.com.

Books by Jo Leigh

Harlequin Blaze

Ms. Match
Sexy Ms. Takes
Shiver
Hotshot
Lying in Bed
All the Right Moves

Three Wicked Nights

One Breathless Night

It's Trading Men

Choose Me
Have Me
Want Me
Seduce Me
Dare Me
Intrigue Me

To get the inside scoop on Harlequin Blaze and its talented writers, be sure to check out BlazeAuthors.com.

All backlist available in ebook format.

Visit the Author Profile page at Harlequin.com for more titles.

To Lena Zimnavoda Khalek,
my amazing niece who has not only been my
source for all things Boston, but is also just plain
wonderful. Love you!

1

KENSEY ROBERTS MADE the short walk from the mansion to her boss's office at a brisk pace. They'd been working out of his Tarrytown, New York, estate for a week now, and normally she enjoyed the leisurely stroll through the garden when she had occasion to meet with him. Not today. She paused outside his door and glanced down at her pressed linen pants and cream-colored blouse.

She'd paid particular attention to how she looked this morning. Her hair was simple, a little wavy now that it was past her shoulders. Applying makeup had been a challenge, but she'd had to do something to hide the fact that she hadn't slept in over twenty-four hours. A final inspection assured her that she looked as cool and polished as usual.

Inside she was a complete mess.

Neil Patterson was sitting behind his immaculate teakwood desk. On any other day, she'd help herself to coffee first, exchange a few pleasantries if he wasn't in the middle of something. Today Kensey headed straight for him and skipped the small talk.

"I hate to spring this on you at the last minute," she said, ignoring the leather chair across from him. Too much adrenaline was shooting through her system. She couldn't sit, hadn't been able to sleep or stomach the thought of food since last night. "I need some time off."

Neil leaned back, eyebrows raised. "Good morning."

Kensey nodded. "Hopefully it will be just a week, so I'll be able to escort the van Gogh to Vienna next month as planned." Her voice, she knew, was well modified, and there was nothing about her expression that signaled anything but calm assurance. This mask had been her saving grace for years. She'd learned how to play a part from the best teacher in the world. "But it's possible I'll be away longer."

Neil didn't ask why. She doubted he thought it had anything to do with the weeks of vacation time she'd never used. He simply waited, his expression as neutral as her own, though she'd bet her Rolex he already knew what was going on. The CEO of The Patterson Group had made his first million at twenty-three and turned that into a billion-dollar empire before he'd hit fifty. Not only was he brilliant, he was careful and he did his research.

He was also the man who'd spotted something worthy enough in her that he'd taken her under his wing four years ago, giving her a life she'd never dreamed possible. Ironically, they'd met over a forgery.

God, Kensey didn't want to disappoint him. But she had something very important to prove.

"I'd wondered if you'd seen this," Neil said, and opened the folder sitting in front of him.

The second she saw the neatly folded copy of the *New York Post* she knew it was over. Her secret was about to unravel. In truth it had started to fray two years ago when Neil had guessed that she had a connection to the Houdini Burglar. But the thefts had stopped by then, and Neil hadn't pressed her to fill in the blanks from her past. He would now, though, and she could hardly blame him.

He slid the paper across his desk. Every part of her wanted to run, but she stayed right where she was, her gaze lowered to the article that could change her life forever.

Art Collector Does a "Houdini" with $10M Degas
by John Witseck

Art lovers around the globe have been stunned by the report that Douglas Foster, highly respected art collector and import/export entrepreneur, is a person of interest in the investigation of a Degas landscape heist.

At nine o'clock Sunday morning, investment banker Clive Seymour discovered his security system disabled and *The Wood*, painted by Edgar Degas, missing from his private collection. Mr. Seymour was alone in his home at the time, although he and longtime associate Foster had dined together the previous evening.

NYPD Detective Sergeant Calvin Brown arrived at the estate at nine-thirty and confirmed that Foster had been Seymour's only dinner guest before Foster left for Manhattan shortly after midnight. According to Mr. Seymour's driver, he dropped Foster off at the Waldorf Astoria where he was staying. Foster, who lives in Paris, had arrived in New York early Saturday afternoon.

When police went to the hotel Sunday morning to pick Mr. Foster up for questioning, he could not be located. His suite had been cleared of his belongings, but a spokesman from the hotel stated Mr. Foster was not due to check out until Tuesday.

Seymour denied that Douglas Foster was the famous art thief dubbed the Houdini Burglar who has eluded authorities across four continents for three decades. Mr. Seymour has declined further comment, though he seemed understandably shocked as the two men have known each other for many years.

Detective Sergeant Brown, a thirty-year veteran of the NYPD white-collar crime division, is confident they will find Mr. Foster and bring him in for questioning. Brown, who will be retiring from the department in three months, has been after the Houdini Burglar for most of his career, although he stated that as of this morning there was no evidence to support the allegations that Foster is involved with the theft.

"Your father, I presume," Neil said, as calm as could be. There wasn't a trace of judgment or censure.

She looked up into his piercing blue eyes and simply nodded. The story hadn't even hit the front page, what with yesterday's oil tanker spill. But it had made page two and the scandal had the fine art world buzzing. Everyone who was anyone knew Douglas Foster. From the time she was young he'd been an A-list party guest.

"He's innocent," Kensey said. "I'm sure of it."

Neil's brows rose. "How would you know that?"

"It's a forgery, a good one, I'll give you that, but it's not perfect."

"You've seen the Degas?"

"No, but I dug up every digital picture of it that was taken after Seymour bought it, and some from the prior owner. Most of the pictures are shadowed or just plain bad. On purpose, I'm thinking. But seeing it up close? Foster would have written it off as a forgery and never given it another thought." No one she knew, and she knew a lot of people in the art world, was better at spotting forgeries. "He taught me just about everything I know."

"Circumstances might have changed," Neil said. "You

haven't seen him in a long time. He's older, slower. It's possible he's lost his touch. It happens."

"He might have slowed down but there's no way he would have taken a forgery. Or for that matter, be so stupid and careless. He was Seymour's only dinner guest. Why on earth would he choose that night to go back and steal the painting? Please. And God knows he doesn't need the money. He has enough to live out three lifetimes in luxury."

Neil smiled. "It's not always about money for people like him. It's the thrill of the chase or the rush of being the smartest and the best. It gets in the blood and clouds people's judgment. So they don't know when to quit."

Kensey's chest hurt. She didn't like the way those unnerving blue eyes studied her so closely. If he'd ever thought she was indeed her father's daughter, or the possibility existed that she could be drawn back to her old life, he would've cut her loose by now.

But no, Neil had always been her champion. What her father never taught her about business or life, Neil Patterson had. He'd invested in her, encouraged her and listened to her opinions.

"All I know is that this thing smells like a setup. Seymour probably realized the painting was a fake ages ago, and knew he couldn't sell it to any of his regular buyers. This con must have dropped into his lap like an early Christmas present. My bet's on the cop. Brown's retiring soon. He's been after the Houdini Burglar for most of his career. He doesn't want to go out looking like a fool."

"A cop? About to retire with a pension?"

"Why not? He's been obsessed."

Neil gave her a slow, considering look. "Fine," he said. "Let's assume you're right. What is it you want to do?"

She tried to relax, her gaze going to the Modigliani hanging behind him. It was one of her favorites, one he'd kept out of circulation far longer than most. She suspected because he knew of her fondness for the painting.

As his curator, she worked up a complete profile for each piece in his vast collection, checking and double-checking the provenances, all of which went into a very complex metadata formula that told them when a piece was ready to go into circulation, and where. Some of the pieces would be marked for sale, while other were to be held on to as an investment. All that mattered to her was that she had the rare and wonderful privilege of seeing the work up close, studying the craft and basking in its pure genius.

"I need to prove he didn't do it," she said, finally sinking into the leather chair. "As long as he's on the run he can't return to his home in Paris or access his accounts. I'm sure he has money stashed away somewhere in case something like this were to ever happen but who knows if he can get to it."

"Do you think he'll try to contact you?"

"No." The thought hadn't even occurred to her. She shook her head. "After ten years without a word? I doubt it."

"You're right. He wouldn't want to involve you."

Kensey stared in disbelief. "Are you serious? He doesn't care about me. A letter, Neil," she said, the pain as sharp now as the day she'd found herself alone in a Swiss hotel. She'd just turned eighteen and was about to start at Yale, which had the best undergraduate fine arts program in the world. She'd been over the moon about it. "Three lines basically telling me to have a nice life was all he left me before he disappeared." He'd also left enough money to finance her Ivy League education, including a master's degree in art restoration at the Istituto Superiore per la Conservazione ed il Restauro in Rome. Plus her Manhattan co-op. She hoped the overtures hadn't eased his guilt one bit. "He's probably forgotten he has a daughter."

Neil hadn't looked away once. But she did, before she could see pity in his eyes. "The smart thing would be to stay away from the investigation," Neil said. "It's not easy to trace you back to that old life, but it can be done. So, why risk it?"

"I don't know." Kensey sighed. "I honestly don't, but... I can't look the other way. I wish I could."

Neil's gaze drifted toward the window and the lush greenery outside. "What's your plan?"

"I don't know that, either." The headache that had been teasing her since four o'clock this morning was making itself known, as it began to throb behind her temples. "If I'm right and he's being framed, the fake painting would have been destroyed by now. The insurance company will have pictures. I still have connections from when I worked as a fraud investigator... I can call in a favor."

Neil stared at her with unforgiving focus. With his thick dark hair and athletic build, the man had the nerve to be great looking. She'd have preferred he wasn't. Not because they had anything going on, but because some people automatically assumed that their relationship was more than professional.

Okay, so they were friends, as well, but that was a far cry from being lovers...

"Do you know how many red flags you'd send up?" Neil asked. "I don't care what anyone owes you, you'll end up under the same microscope as Foster."

"I hadn't thought that far ahead," she admitted. "But you're right. I need to be careful." She exhaled slowly, embarrassed at how foolish she sounded. "I can't let this go, Neil. I can't. He's in his late fifties. He can't spend the rest of his life in prison. Even if he gets off, the authorities will be watching him. He'd be forced to retire. So I wouldn't feel guilty helping him."

Neil nodded. "I agree something's off. It wouldn't surprise me if he has been set up. But he's not my concern. You are."

Kensey smiled. "Thank you." Of course he would think of her first. She'd never wanted him to be involved, but now that he was, she was incredibly grateful. "I mean it. I don't know where I'd be without you. I hope you understand that I have to do this."

"Time isn't on your side, Kensey. You'd have to work fast. Once the police arrest him and have enough to indict him, the prosecution will start digging deep. And I don't think they're going to dither on this one. Too many rich, interested people involved. No judge will consider bail, since he's the poster boy for flight risk. And once he's in Sing Sing, he's going to stay there."

Her heart squeezed so tightly it took her by surprise. She never would have guessed that helping her father would matter so much to her. "I can't tell if you're encouraging me to get moving, or trying to get me to drop it."

"I know you better than to think you'd do that." He rose and walked over to the coffee service on his credenza. After filling his own mug, he held out the carafe to her.

She shook her head. God, all she needed was more caffeine added to the adrenaline racing through her body.

"I know you have something in mind," he said. "Tell me what it is."

"I don't have a plan. Not really—" The idea Kensey had entertained at five o'clock this morning seemed completely insane now. If she told Neil about it, he would probably have her committed on the spot. No, first he'd fire her, then he'd call a psychiatrist to send men in white coats to haul her off to some sterile institution with cheap hotel art on the walls. Kensey sighed. "I could steal the original myself."

Anyone else might've spit out his coffee. Neil swallowed and set the mug down on his desk, then sat. "You don't know who has the Degas."

"We've both heard the rumors."

"*Rumors* being the operative word."

Kensey studied her boss. His brows lowered, he wasn't quite frowning, more like he was deep in thought. She was encouraged by the fact that he hadn't told her outright it was a ridiculous idea.

"You and Ian Holstrom used to be business partners," she said. "Do *you* think he could have a private collection of stolen masterpieces?"

"We parted company over twenty years ago. Hard to say what he's into now."

"Is he capable of such a thing?"

Neil's smile held no humor. "He wasn't always narcissistic and greedy. We made a lot of money very quickly and Ian figured that entitled him to a seat among Boston's elite. But he was crass, always talking about how rich he was. People didn't like him. They still don't, no matter how much expensive art he acquires. So, yes, I can see him wanting to stick it to everyone by hording stolen art for his own amusement, but I can also see how the rumors might have gotten started out of disdain for the man."

"But since the Degas hasn't been seen in seven years, only the forgery, it is possible Holstrom has it, right?"

"It's also possible Seymour's painting isn't a forgery."

Kensey didn't blink. "I'm not wrong. And I don't have any other leads."

Neil sighed. "Look, you can't break into his house. Holstrom has top-notch security. He's an arms dealer and defense contractor, for God's sake." Neil held up a hand when Kensey tried to interrupt. "However, in addition to his love of art, he has an insatiable appetite for fine wine and beautiful women..."

"Okay," she said. "So, what are you thinking?"

His smile relaxed her, but not because it was reassuring. Most people found that particular smile to be comforting. Fools, all of them. Her boss was wickedly smart and when he flashed that easy grin, she knew the axe was about to fall.

She had no idea what had caused the eventual rift between him and Holstrom; she could only thank her lucky stars that Neil was on her side.

"First of all, stealing the Degas isn't the answer. I assume you meant you would turn it over to the authorities," Neil said with a faint smile. "That won't prove Foster didn't steal it."

About to argue, she realized he was right. "I have to prove the original has been in Holstrom's possession all along."

Neil nodded. "Unfortunately, that will still require access to his estate," he said, running a critical gaze over Kensey. "But I don't imagine it would take much for you to catch Holstrom's attention."

She took no offense. Not with Neil. But the thought of using her sexuality to snare the man made her shudder inside, although she knew she could do it, if that was what it would take. "Go on."

"His office is in Boston where there happens to be a major security convention next week. He'll begin the night before the conference officially opens with a party at The Four Seasons or the Mandarin Oriental hotel where he'll parade his wealth like Caligula. Business will be done there, but the point will be to show off how rich and powerful he is. I'll make a call, get you registered at the conference and put you together with a friend of mine. Knowing Sam, she'll be very helpful. By then I'll have gotten as much information on Holstrom as I'm able to, and we'll go from there. You should know I can't get you on the list for the party."

Kensey nodded, marveling at how much her boss knew about Holstrom, but also wondering just how much Neil Patterson knew about her.

She'd said very little about her past, so she didn't see how he could understand the nature of her early relationship with her father. How he'd taught her to be more than a decoy when she was younger. He'd pressed her to learn three languages, to take gymnastics and keep herself limber. She'd added martial arts, and he'd approved. And she'd sat at his feet, learning to become any character he needed, from naive waif to budding seductress. Not that he had let anything happen to her, but she'd been a very convincing actress.

He was meticulous. Every heist was studied until he understood everything he'd need to grab what he was after. Timetables, security systems, safes. The reason Douglas Foster had never been caught was that he never left his exit strategies to luck.

All of his expertise had been passed down to her. She'd believed, up until the day he disappeared from her life, that he'd been molding her into his protégé.

Even now her blood pulsed through her system like a maelstrom, the call to danger as familiar as breathing, but far more exciting. If she pulled this off…if she proved Douglas Foster innocent, he would see who she'd become. That she didn't need him at all.

2

"You're going to miss your flight, and you'll feel horrible and probably do something self-destructive like flirt with someone wildly unsuitable who'll end up stealing your wallet."

"That happened one time." Logan McCabe frowned at his sister. His advice to anyone who wanted a nice, sane life? Don't have a sister. Actually, it should be don't have *his* sister. Lisa was newly engaged and particularly chipper these days. He couldn't wait to get to Boston. "Would you stop interrupting? I just want to make sure I've crossed all the *t*'s."

"Now you're blaming me for your jitters? What happened to the old nerves of steel? Mr. Former CIA Covert Ops—"

He looked up from his business proposal to catch her gaze. "Lisa, you know better."

"I'm sorry," she said, wincing. "I won't do that again. I swear."

No one else was in the office. He knew she hadn't meant anything by what she said. But he worried that some day she'd kid around in front of the wrong person and they'd both be in serious trouble. The blame fell on him. He and Lisa were close, but he'd had no business telling her about his work for the CIA. He hadn't told her anything specific, but he should have kept his mouth shut, period.

She rose from one of the visitors' chairs in his Lower East Side office. The furniture was fine, if you didn't care about comfort. But then anyone sitting across from him in this office wouldn't give a damn about comfort or style or anything so trivial. He met clients elsewhere. The office was reserved for veterans like himself. The hardcore, superbly trained members of the Navy SEALs, Green Berets, Delta Force, Twenty-fourth Special Tactics, or Army Rangers. Some of whom, like him, had been recruited by the CIA to take on high-risk missions the military couldn't perform. But the guys he helped, the ones who were just returning from active duty, all shared the monumental task of learning how to live among civilians. Becoming a civilian was, as far as Logan was concerned, impossible.

It had taken a long time, but finally he'd realized he could utilize his experience to make a difference. For himself. And for the others who had the best training in the world, but no place to put their skills to work. "I wish you were coming with me," he told Lisa, mostly to let her know he wasn't pissed. "Each time I talk to Sam it seems she's leaped ahead another ten years. Her equipment is so advanced it would blow your mind. And she's one of the best when it comes to spyware."

"I'm more interested in that apartment of hers. It sounds very sci-fi."

"It's still a prototype, but yeah, it should be interesting. Hey, what time is it?"

"Too tired to turn your wrist? You've got an hour before you have to be at the airport."

Rolling his eyes wasn't something he did with his sister. He'd never get anything else done if he started. But the urge never died.

"You want to rehearse your presentation again?" she asked. "Or go over your pitch for Holstrom?"

Logan had agreed to give a talk so that he could get the word out about his model for staffing, but now he was sorry. It was critical to win the security contract from Ian Holstrom. The rest could wait. "If I lost my PowerPoint tomorrow, I'd be able to give the spiel in my sleep."

"Does that mean you're worried about Holstrom?"

He nodded. "There are two other top outfits gunning for the contract, and both of them are established in the field."

"You're established," she said. "You've overseen three major operations already, and you've only been doing this for two years."

Logan leaned back until he felt the lumbar support on his big leather chair settle into the sweet spot. "Two years versus ten?"

"Didn't you tell me Holstrom wants new blood?"

"That's what he said. I have no idea if he meant it."

"Presuming he didn't, what would you do?"

He gave her question some thought, but didn't share his suspicion that Holstrom might be blowing smoke about the competition. Yeah, the two other companies had great track records but they didn't have the kind of field experience Logan had, nor did they have his insight into the type of man with the skills of a special-ops soldier. Holstrom had been clear that he wanted only the best for the most critical jobs. Not just a bunch of mercenaries. But he didn't blame Holstrom for using the threat of competitors. That was just business. But in case it wasn't a ploy, Logan was determined not to get too smug. Too many people were depending on him.

"Nothing very different," he said in answer to Lisa. "I'd

put more emphasis on the fact that I only recruit spec-ops vets for critical assignments. That everyone on the team has mandatory counseling and ongoing training in tactics, advanced firearms and physical fitness."

"Okay, then. You've thought of everything, and you'll blow his socks off," she said. "Now, listen up. You'll be in Boston for six days. You're going to want to change your ticket to come back early, but please don't. The last time you took some real time off was…wait a minute. I'll remember soon. Oh, yeah, freshman year at MIT? When you and your friends went to Cozumel?"

"Yes. Okay. I get it."

"No," she said, and now she was standing in front of him, her hands planted above his big desk calendar, her face too close for comfort. "I don't think you do," she said. "Dr. Price told you to take some time off. I'd bet all your money that he meant more than two lousy days. You need to take care of yourself if you're going to take care of your veterans, Logan. Be an example, not a cautionary tale. Remember what you told me when I was getting back on my feet? You gave me the very touching brotherly advice to get laid once in a while."

Logan smiled. "What makes you think I'm not?"

"Oh, please. You wouldn't be such a pain in the ass if you were." She gave him that soft look of sisterly concern that made him want to go to the airport early. "Besides, how is Mike ever going to learn how to take over operations if you never leave him alone to run things?"

"Fine." He rubbed a hand over his face. Mike, a former army ranger, had been with them a year now and was adjusting exceptionally well.

"Give me your word you won't find a reason to come back early."

"I can't do that. But I promise I'll do my best to get some R & R."

"All right. As long as you're serious about making the effort."

He knew she was right. Working nonstop for as long as he had wasn't in his best interest. But, truth be told, he hadn't figured out how to turn off in the way she meant. It wasn't that simple. Years of covert work where there were no days off—no seconds off—had instilled in him pathways of thinking, of being. Going to the supermarket could be an ordeal. The first year back he hadn't been able to make it through a quick shop without wanting to pull his weapon or call for backup. Things were much better now, but not easy.

Lisa understood, though. She was a former cop and had difficulty in the same arena. But now that she was with Daniel, she seemed more at ease.

"I know you love me to pieces," she said. "We'll be fine here. And you'll do great. Oh, and by the way, please tell the famous Sam that I'm going with you next time to stay in that smart apartment of hers."

"Neither of us could afford to stay there after this beta test phase is finished."

"Way to burst every balloon in the world, Logan."

"I'm valued for my ability to ruin people's day."

"You're valued because you're amazing," she said.

He had no idea where his kid sister got her ideas. He wasn't amazing. He was simply good at his work. Because he remembered what it had been like to have no purpose. No use for his skills. It was like being in solitary confinement without hope of parole.

BY THE TIME Logan reached Boston, he couldn't wait to grab a hot shower and drink a nice cold beer. Even so, after he got out of the cab he paused to take in his surroundings. The street itself consisted of old brownstone row houses, except for Sam's place. Her building was set back, with a brick walkway and heavy trees that lowered the June warmth by at least ten degrees. Sam was lucky to have found it.

He'd heard from his college buddy Rick that the apartment was fully intuitive, and damn, Logan needed something to help him relax. The short flight from New York had made him grumpy as hell. He hated commercial flying. Everything was too crowded, too expensive, too noisy.

And while he'd tried the mindfulness exercises the company's shrink had taught him, the kid behind him kicking his seat the entire flight had turned his meditation into a long list of reasons why he should never have children.

As soon as he opened Sam's front door, perfectly placed lights came on in the apartment. The temperature was a few degrees cooler than outside, without a trace of humidity. He immediately liked the open floor plan with the foyer spilling into a room that was both modern and welcoming, with expensive-looking artwork on the walls. But the art couldn't compete with the magic happening inside the walls—they changed color as he walked through the sleekly furnished living room.

Just to make sure he hadn't lost his mind, which was a legitimate concern, he went back to the marble foyer. Sure enough, the wall colors shifted from a pale blue to a paler blue, then a faint green and finally beige. When he returned to the living room, it was different again. This time the walls turned from pale pink to violet.

It wasn't just a gimmick, either. Sam had explained that the walls contained body sensors, and Logan really did feel calmer as he walked into the open kitchen. It was high-end in every way, and when he opened the pantry door, he realized he could stay there for a month without missing a single meal.

Sam was going to make a fortune with this place. He found the master suite at the end of a short hallway. It was huge and the bed was a California king. Man, it just kept getting better. He dumped his duffel bag on the bed and put his computer case on the floor.

Goddamn, one look at the shower insured he'd be taking his time. No door to speak of, a boatload of sparkly tile, and more jets than La Guardia. All that was missing was an ice-cold beer…which was probably in that industrial-sized refrigerator in the kitchen. He'd have to go grab that first.

Yep, he found the beer. His favorite brand, too. There was a lot of delicious-looking food in the fridge, but there was only one thing he cared about at the moment. He popped the top and took a drink, a burst of hops hitting his nose. When he lowered the can, he froze.

A woman stood in the living room staring back at him.

Tall. Blonde. Gorgeous.

And naked. Almost.

A white towel covered most of her breasts, but if she bent in pretty much any direction…

Looking away would be the right thing to do. Only, he didn't know who she was or why she was there.

Logan wiped his mouth. "I think you might be in the wrong apartment."

"No," she said, weirdly calm for a woman wearing only a towel and facing a strange man. "I'm sure I'm just where I'm supposed to be."

"Well, hell, you'd better be a hologram." Logan nearly choked at the crazy thought. "Although Sam did say the apartment came with everything."

"Excuse me?" The woman narrowed her eyes. They looked green but he had to get closer to be sure.

"Are you…real?" He moved a step toward her. With

all of Sam's tech voodoo he honestly couldn't tell. "Can I touch you?"

"Not if you want to live to finish that beer."

Logan smiled. "Sam knows I like feisty women."

"I wish she'd warned me that you're delusional."

Okay, so she knew Sam or at least that Sam was a she. "What am I supposed to think with you greeting me in a towel?" He checked out her legs. Man, they were long. "For the record, no towel would've been better," he said and took a pull of beer. Then swallowed quickly. "Wait. It was Lisa. She sent you, didn't she?"

"No one sent me." She inched back, daring him with a glare. "I'm beginning to seriously hope you aren't Logan."

"Guilty as charged." He didn't know what to think at the moment. Except that since she knew Sam and who he was, she probably wasn't trespassing. "What's your name?"

"Kensey. I'm here for the conference but I couldn't find a room anywhere in the city," she said, shifting slightly to her right. "You're early."

If she moved another centimeter, he'd be seeing her religion. It was bad enough that the image of her shapely legs was now burned into his brain, and all of his conversational abilities had been overtaken by the potential movement of that small towel.

He needed that shower ASAP. Or ten minutes of privacy. Either one would do.

"Who's Lisa?"

"My kid sister."

"And you think she sent you a hooker?" The woman raised an eyebrow. A lovely eyebrow. All the parts of her that he could see were lovely. He doubted he'd ever used or thought that particular word before, but this gorgeous blonde in the tiny towel brought out the poet in him. Among other things. "Interesting family," she said, with a look that didn't just dismiss him. It dismissed him with prejudice.

"I don't have to play nice with you," he said. "I have no idea who you are. Until I speak to the owner of this apartment, I get to assume anything that makes sense to me." He moved a few inches to the right and said, "Call Sam."

Just like that, a screen appeared on the wall behind her. It looked like a large computer monitor with Sam's company logo in the center. He could hear a phone ringing, the call signal created by the Skype program.

Seconds later, Sam herself was in the center of the screen. Her eyes widened as she got a load of Kensey. "Damn it, Logan. I've been trying to reach you. What the hell's wrong with your cell phone?"

"Nothing."

"Look again."

He retrieved his phone from his jacket. It was off. He'd switched it off on the plane in a vain attempt to get some sleep, and had forgotten to turn it back on. That was worrisome on several levels. He turned the damn thing on. "Why were you trying to reach me?"

His cell phone beeped five times in a row. He slid it into his pocket while avoiding looking at the seminaked woman beside him.

"To tell you that you'd have company for the week. I assume you've introduced yourselves?"

"Not exactly."

"Look, Logan, she's one of the good guys. I know I promised you the place to yourself, but this is kind of an emergency, so please be okay with it."

He hadn't decided if he was happy or not, but if Sam said Kensey was good people, he believed her. "You gonna be around?"

Sam frowned. "Aren't I always?"

Sam wasn't her usual cheerful self. Normally, she

never left a conversation before filling him in on what she was up to. In detail. He rarely understood what she was talking about because Sam was in a class by herself. He wrote her mood off to the security conference. She had a lot of spyware—not just for computers, but for equipment that men like him needed if they wanted to stay alive. She must be up to her neck in clients. "I'll call you later. And Sam? The place is unreal."

That made her smile. The definition on the wall monitor was so incredible that he could count the freckles on her nose.

She turned her attention to Kensey. "Sorry about this," she said. "Yesterday and today have been nuts. I'm normally completely on top of things."

"I understand. No problem."

"You'll get along great with Logan. He's interesting. And funny." She glanced at something behind her. "Sorry, I've got to run."

With that, she vanished from the monitor. And the monitor went with her.

"Satisfied?" his guest asked.

"So you know Sam. And you're here for the conference?"

"Yes."

"Who do you work for?"

"Neil—" She pushed the hair off her right shoulder, making her appear even more naked. "My boss and I have parted ways. I'm currently freelancing. I understand you're military?"

"I was, but we've also parted ways."

"Do tell," she said, moving her hips half a millimeter to the right. "I can't wait to see if this is the part where you get interesting and/or funny."

Good thing he'd had a lifetime of training with his sis-

ter so he was able to sidestep that comment like a crack
on the sidewalk. "Sure you're not chilly in that outfit?"

Her lips lifted a fraction of a second before settling
back into a straight line. "If it bothers you, I'll go change
right now."

"No. Nope. Doesn't bother me at all." He smiled. Tried
to remember what she'd asked him about. And wondered
how he could move over to where he'd be covered from
the erection down without making it obvious that was
what he was doing.

"How was your breakup with the military?" she asked.

"Amicable. For the most part."

"I'm guessing you're going to the conference because
you're in the security business?"

He nodded. "Cliché as that is. Even civilians need pro-
tection."

"That's very noble of you."

"It keeps bread on the table and beer in the fridge.
What about you? I think you would make one hell of a
personal guard."

She laughed, her eyes bright with surprise. Green.
Definitely green. "I'd be terrible at it. I've got no training at all."

He couldn't help shaking his head. With those looks
and that insane calm in a situation that would make anyone else run for cover, he imagined she'd do just fine.
"What do you have training in?"

"You know what? I'm getting chilly. So, we'll talk
again, Logan…?"

"McCabe."

"Nice to meet you," she said. "But the reason I came
out here was to get a snack. However, I'm reasonably
certain that my derriere is not completely covered. I'd
appreciate it if you turned away and closed your eyes."

He let out a deep breath. "Depends. Have you ever heard of Pliny the Elder?"

"Ancient Roman big shot?" The way she looked at him, as if he were a complete wacko made him relax completely. "Wrote the first encyclopedia?"

"Yes. And if you see any bottles in the fridge that look like this—" he turned his beer so she could see the name "—they're for me."

She sighed and added a little head shake. "Awesome. A guy who doesn't like to share. Fine. I won't touch your beer."

Walking casually toward the fridge, as if she went to work five days a week wearing a towel and nothing else, she passed him, close and slow. He got a whiff of something dark, sweet and hot. Then she twirled her finger for him to turn his back.

Sadly, he did as she asked. "I'm serious about that beer."

The pantry door swung open behind him. Something rustled, the door closed and then the fridge opened and closed in quick succession. Kensey walked by him again, leaving her scent in her wake.

Damn, if he didn't want to lick her like a popsicle.

"I'm serious about you keeping your eyes shut," she said.

"They're shut tight. Just slam your bedroom door so I'll know the coast is clear."

He didn't hear any footsteps, so he followed the sound of what he thought might be her munching on potato chips.

Then in the next moment, a door slammed, and if he wasn't mistaken, the lock was slipped into place.

He needed to have a private talk with Sam. But not before he did something about the burgeoning problem in his jeans.

3

KENSEY WAITED UNTIL the lock was fully engaged before she let go of the breath she'd been holding. From the second she'd seen Logan, she'd been consumed with the thought that her towel would fall. It wasn't tightened all that well. But she'd just stepped out of the shower and hadn't expected him for another two hours.

She found a thick white spa robe hanging in the closet and slipped into it, and nearly squeezed herself to death tying the belt. Then she turned to look at the wall. "Call—" She stopped. Sam was busy.

They had spoken before Kensey had left New York, and the woman had explained a little about the apartment and who she'd be sharing it with. But Kensey was in no way prepared for the reality of walls changing colors and a shower that had given her more pleasure than her last three dates combined.

And she sure as hell hadn't been prepared for Logan.

A beep sounded behind her. She turned to see a monitor on the wall with text telling her it was Sam. Kensey quickly accepted the call.

"Hi, Kensey," Sam said, from the wall.

It was so weird to see her image right there, larger than life. "You went to Hogwarts, didn't you?"

"I wish," Sam said. "I'm sorry about Logan. I left him several messages, but I was too swamped with appointments to follow up. I hope he didn't give you too much of a scare."

"Scare? No. It was fine, although I might've avoided meeting him wearing only a towel."

"I don't know how you managed to stay so calm. I would've just died." Sam's cheeks reddened. "Of course I don't look like you."

"Stop it." Kensey shook her head. "Don't underestimate yourself. Oh, and speaking of looks, you couldn't have warned me that Logan is hotter than hell?"

"I guess I've known him too long. He just looks like Logan to me. One of my college buddies. But yeah, all the girls back at MIT loved him." Sam wrinkled her nose. "Huh. Now that I think about it, all the guys I hung out with were pretty good looking."

"Now that you think about it?" Kensey laughed. "Did you ever look away from your computer?" But what did she know? She had no friends at all, except Neil. She'd always been so worried about guarding her past that she hadn't exactly welcomed new people into her life.

Well, after this week, maybe she'd make some friends with her fellow inmates at Bedford Hills Correctional Facility.

"Yeah, a group of us hung out. I was the only computer geek. Logan studied political science, forensics and languages. He speaks four. Anyway, our friendship was mostly accidental but it turned out to be one of the best parts of university life for me."

Kensey started to ask which languages, but thought better of it. She couldn't think of Logan as anything but a temporary roommate. In fact, she couldn't afford to think about him at all, so she changed the subject. "The body sensors you mentioned yesterday…that's what's causing the walls to change color, right?"

Sam nodded. "They're heat, movement and tone sensors that can pick up if you're having a rough night's sleep and cue up something soothing to listen to. Or if you're anxious, they'll surround you in calming colors, scents and sounds," she said patiently, though there seemed to be a lot of activity buzzing around her. "I'm sorry. This week is kind of hectic."

"It's fine, Sam. Really. I'll figure things out. Thanks," Kensey said. "For everything."

"Listen, I want you to know if you need anything, you can reach me pretty much all the time. Even if I'm at the exhibition hall. I promise we'll meet in person at some point."

"I look forward to it."

"Me, too." Sam smiled and disappeared, leaving the wall just a wall.

Except it wasn't just a wall—it could read her moods. It was all so crazy. She would've loved being here under different circumstances. And Logan with those sexy hazel eyes? Under different circumstances, she would've loved meeting him.

Sharing the apartment would have been much easier if he'd been unattractive. And meeting him for the first time while she was wearing only a towel? Fantastic. At least they wouldn't have much interaction this evening. She had to get ready to crash Holstrom's reception at the Mandarin Oriental.

Kensey flipped on the light and walked into the large closet, a nice hint of cedar rising from the floor. She hadn't noticed the scent before. Probably because she'd hung everything as quickly as she'd grabbed and purchased the clothes a few hours ago.

She looked at the long row of clothing: dresses, skirts, blouses, pants. All of it gorgeous. And sexy. Way sexier than anything she normally wore. But then, these were costumes. More expensive than anything she'd ever owned, and integral to the character she was about to play.

She'd been worried, at first, after she'd done a bit more research about Holstrom, that she wouldn't be able to get his attention. From what she'd read, he didn't seem to go for tall blondes, but that wasn't enough to dissuade her. She knew he loved being the center of attention, and, tonight, she would bring that to him in spades. Then, after he was hooked like a trout, she would vanish into the night.

And come back here to have her coronary in private.

She decided she would go with the beautiful flowing number by Donna Karan for tonight's party. The dress was the color of turmeric and clay, strapless and tight around her chest, with an airy, semitransparent skirt that flowed past her ankles. She hoped it was enough to get her into Holstrom's reception and catch his eye. If he proved challenging, there were a few things she could do. The simplest of which would be to drop her small clutch at his feet. Eye contact would be easy once he picked it up for her.

God, all this reminded her of her father. Wherever he was. Before he'd taken a runner, she and her father had lived the high life. They went to extravagant parties and ate at the best restaurants in New York City, Paris and Rome. The memories made her heart race—but not in an entirely good way. Believing she could get Holstrom to show her his secret collection had seemed easier two hundred miles away in Tarrytown. But it wasn't as if she had much of a choice.

After applying a good deal more makeup than usual and slicking her hair completely off her face, she checked her new dramatic look in the mirror. She decided against wearing any jewelry. It took her a minute to believe she was staring at her own reflection, and then she was ready to go, slippery clutch in hand.

"Hey," Logan said, as he walked down the hallway from his bedroom. "I'm going to order a pizza. Want in?"

He blinked at her. Damn, he was good looking. The way his jeans fit him, the V of a tight waist and broad shoulders. His sun-streaked brown hair was slightly damp and slicked back. She would have loved to stick around and see if he was everything Sam claimed, but she couldn't.

"I've got someplace to be," she said.

He returned the toe-to-head scan. "Wow."

Kensey smiled. Managed to look flattered but not overly so. "Thanks. Pizza would've been good, though," she said, and probably shouldn't have. "But now, I've got to run."

"Have you ordered a taxi yet?"

"Yes. Thanks."

The way his gaze moved down her body, slowly, then lingered on where the silky fabric grazed her thighs made her want to squeeze them together. If Logan's reaction was any indication, the dress was doing its job.

His dark brows lowered. "Did you forget—" He met her eyes, cleared his throat and looked away. "Have a good time."

Fairly certain she knew what he'd been about to say, she tried not to laugh. The flow of the dress was very tricky. Depending on the angle, the lighting, the motion of her body, it appeared as if she might be naked underneath the translucent fabric.

He turned around and headed back toward his room, the walls on both sides turning varying shades of red as he hurried down the hallway.

THE TAXI RIDE had been good for her, a way to settle and get comfortable in her role. Logan's reaction had helped. She knew she'd picked the perfect dress. The slight alteration she'd made to the bodice made her breasts look larger than they were. But undeniably, it was the stunning gossamer fabric and what it revealed that would help her pass the next test.

A tall beefy man in a black suit stood at the entrance to the banquet room where Holstrom was hosting his reception. Thirtysomething, with hard features, she could tell he wasn't an ordinary rent-a-cop. A member of Holstrom's private security team, she imagined. This might not be as easy as she'd hoped.

"Good evening. May I see your invitation, please?"

Standing tall but looking at him through her eyelashes, she pretended to check inside her small clutch. She sighed with a hint of impatience, then snapped the catch shut and dipped her finger and thumb into her bodice, between her breasts.

The man tried not to stare. But he couldn't seem to help himself.

Her smile turned pensive, not that he'd noticed. Interesting, because he seemed a little old and seasoned to be quite so mesmerized, but she'd take it. Of course she didn't have the invitation, but she did have a tube of lipstick, which she pulled out. "I know I didn't leave it at the hotel," she said. "It may have come loose but I'm sure it's here. I'd folded it so it would fit."

She went in for a second time.

Kensey could have sworn his body had tensed, but his expression remained unchanged.

"It's fine, ma'am. I'm sure you're on the list." He gestured to the open door. "Please, go ahead."

She smiled and walked confidently into the elegant

Mandarin Oriental ballroom, grabbed a flute of champagne from a passing waiter and sipped from it as she took stock of the party she'd just crashed.

She'd wondered why Holstrom wasn't entertaining in one of the more intimate suites. Now she understood. There had to be over a hundred people in attendance, plenty of strutting men with beautiful women close at hand. Premium champagne and chilled bottles of imported vodka were on display, as were six young women in tiny outfits who were extolling the virtues of Holstrom's battle tanks, RPGs, submachine guns, sniper rifles and Lord knows what else.

To make it seem even more like something out of a movie, upbeat elevator music played softly in the background, and there was a ridiculous ratio of waiters to guests. The people who had been invited to this reception wouldn't be walking the exhibit hall during the conference. And they'd definitely not be attending any sessions. She doubted that there was one guest in that room who wasn't worth at least a billion dollars. In Holstrom's case, it was many billions.

More than half the men were Middle Eastern and she recognized a few bigwigs from Eastern Europe. Their plus-ones were mostly American women in classy but slightly immodest clothes, although there were two women in gorgeous abayas sitting in one of the tidy group lounges.

And there he was.

Ian Holstrom, five-foot-eleven with a suspiciously rich head of dark hair, was as trim as an athlete and dressed like a king. To say he was tailored missed the mark. His suit fit him so perfectly it outshined every other Western man in the room.

At least she'd been forewarned about him. Virtually

every photo of him played up his massive ego. In the flesh, he wore his superiority like a cape.

She had to nail her entrance. But playing the part of a woman who bore no resemblance to herself would be even more challenging.

Knowing that somewhere in Boston, probably in his home, there could be a treasure trove of stolen masterpieces from around the world, gave her the courage to do whatever it took to get to him. And, of course, thinking about her father being wrongly accused...

No, that didn't help.

Pushing aside all thoughts to focus exclusively on her prey, Kensey lingered near the door, waiting for the perfect moment to make her entrance. It took a while, but she understood patience. Finally, Holstrom was at the far end of the room, and she was directly in his sight line. She pushed her shoulders back and began her walk.

The liquid silk of her dress caressed her body with fluid grace out behind her and in between her legs. Using a model's runway strut, she thrust out her pelvis as she took extra long steps, which wasn't easy in five-inch heels. But it worked.

A slight hush fell, and she sensed that lots of people were watching her, but all she cared about was one pair of eyes.

There. She'd done it. He hadn't just looked, he'd stared. Looked her up and down, from head to toe with revisits to her crotch and her breasts. They were her tools tonight, and she was glad she'd kept up with her martial arts and gymnastics.

Just as she'd hoped, Holstrom walked to her those last five footsteps, abandoning the brunette at his side. "And who might you be?" he asked. His voice was half an octave too high to be truly sexy. She'd bet that killed him.

She put out her hand. "Kensington Roberts," she said. "My friends call me Kensey."

Being a gentleman, or a reasonable facsimile, he took her hand in his. "Tell me, Kensey, are you here with someone?"

"No. I came here tonight to meet you. To introduce myself."

"Oh?" he said. "And why is that?"

"Because I've heard a lot about you. I was here at the conference, anyway, and I thought, why not?"

He smiled. Maybe because he finally realized he was still holding her hand. He let her go, but he took his time.

Jesus, what was she doing? Her father had probably done business with this son of a bitch. Sold him stolen paintings so that Holstrom could get off knowing he was the only one who could ever look at them.

"I truly am here for the conference," she said. "Security is part of my job."

"Are you a bodyguard?"

She laughed softly. "Not quite. I'm a curator." Looking around as if she'd seen nothing but him before now, she gasped, subtly. "This room is amazing. I've heard about your parties, and I swore I would find out if the rumors were true."

He raised his eyebrows. "Rumors?"

"That you want only the best of the best. That you never settle, or skimp. That you are incredibly discerning, especially when it comes to art and wine."

He smiled, but his gaze had become less enchanted and more curious. "A curator? For a museum? A private collector?"

"I just left a job, so I'm currently freelancing." She smiled shyly as she let her gaze move down his body. His suit was even more impressive up close. "I must be holding you up," she said, slowly lifting her gaze until she met his light eyes. "I hope to see you at the conference."

"You aren't leaving so soon." With a slight frown he glanced toward the entrance. "You put a lot of effort into getting into a very private party. And you've cost a fool his job."

"Oh, no. Please don't do that," she said. "I'm quite sure he'll never make that mistake again."

"No, he won't. Not in my organization. But surely you want to stay and have some vodka and caviar." He signaled for a waiter. "The blinis and caviar are excellent."

"Thank you." She took a step toward the door, pleased to see men were still eyeing her. Their envious looks would play well to Holstrom's ego. "Everything looks wonderful, but I'm meeting someone for dinner."

He didn't try to persuade her further but started walking with her. "In case we don't meet at the conference, where can I reach you? Perhaps you'll allow me to take you for drinks or to dinner. I'm assuming you're not from Boston?"

"No, I'm not." She took out a card with only her name and cell number, printed yesterday for this very purpose, and gave it to him.

They'd reached the door where the guard remained at his post. Kensey touched Holstrom's arm. "Please don't fire him, Ian," she said, her voice a breathy whisper close to his ear. "It's my fault and I'd feel awful."

A slow smile curved Holstrom's mouth. "A beautiful woman with a soft heart," he said. "Max is one of my best men. I suppose I can overlook his lapse in judgment."

"Thank you." Kensey pulled her hand back but not before Holstrom gave it a light squeeze.

She thought he might be watching her head for the elevator, but she didn't look back. She didn't feel comfortable until she was downstairs, waiting for the doorman to flag her cab.

Once she was on her way, her thoughts went to Logan instead of reviewing what had happened with Holstrom.

She imagined Logan instead of Ian in that amazing suit, and that made her shift on her seat, and then she imagined him without the suit.

Which she had to stop doing before she fogged up all the windows.

She decided it would be foolish not to find out more about him. Despite Sam's assurances that he was one of the good guys, Kensey didn't know him from Adam. And considering she would be spending the next several days with him, it would be to her advantage to spend some time with him, learn whatever she could. The apartment was large, but there was always the risk of being overheard or of him finding something that raised questions.

She needed to make sure he wasn't a threat.

And there was no law against having a nice time while she did it.

4

LOGAN STOOD AT the entrance to the Security Conference and Exhibition and realized everyone had gotten there early to beat the crowds. Oh, well, he'd known there was no way this shindig wasn't going to be massive.

The security business had grown beyond anyone's expectations over the past ten years, which was good for his personal future and not so great for the world. But this conference covered everything from security for presidents and popes to outfitting classrooms and private bedrooms with the latest security measures.

He would take his time today, check out some of the new technology…although he doubted anything on display could match what he'd seen back at Sam's apartment. Her presentation was going to make one hell of a big splash on closing day, especially with the debut of a completely new kind of minicam. But Sam was specialized and he needed a lot more than what she could provide.

What had begun as a small security startup to ease him back into civilian life had grown into something far bigger than he'd ever imagined. Big enough to employ some of his fellow vets and give them an opportunity to do something worthwhile.

Which was why he needed that contract from Holstrom. While Logan preferred to operate independently, it would take years before he had the corporate and government contacts and the credibility that Holstrom had established. The timing was perfect. Holstrom had made his mark and a hell of a lot of money selling weapons. Last year he'd branched out to the security business, and while he was savvy and already doing well, he still had a lot to learn about navigating the intricacies of working on foreign soil.

That's where Logan could shine. He had firsthand experience and knowledge of operating in the field. He also personally knew a lot of excellent, highly trained men well enough to identify their strengths, their weaknesses and whether they were mentally capable of being sent back into the field. His insight also enabled him to place them in positions for which they'd be best suited.

Unfortunately, being former black ops couldn't help him land clients. As far as politicians and most every other American were concerned, soldiers like him—men and women who worked in the shadows—didn't exist beyond Hollywood. And that nice and tidy fallacy worked very well for the secrecy coveted by a certain arm of the CIA.

He didn't regret his patriotic service, nor had he been looking for glory. But it sure as hell would've been useful to list his experience on his résumé. Potential clients would be lining up to have access to someone who'd been a member of the world's most elite team of professional soldiers. On the other hand, he'd have to explain why he'd left the CIA. And that was something he didn't want to think about, much less discuss with anyone.

Logan hadn't gotten past that one yet. It didn't seem to matter that his final mission was a failure. He had his target in his sights, but the kill shot would have taken out a small child—collateral damage. He couldn't pull the trigger. The target wasn't even a credible threat, but that didn't matter. Another sniper had taken the shot in Logan's stead. The child had died. And he was done.

Luckily he didn't think about it as often anymore, and he wasn't about to let the past cloud his judgment now. He owed it to himself and his brothers to give the opportunity to subcontract for Holstrom his full attention. So far Logan had used only a handful of special-ops vets for domestic cases, but word had been spreading in its intricate way through the legion of tier-one special operatives that he was expanding. And now he had over a hundred interested men ready to sign. All of them eager and ready to roll. It all came down to securing enough funds. His personal savings and portfolio would only take him so far.

The first booth that caught his attention had night vision scopes sporting new technology that made them easier to use. He got carried away and made it to only two more booths before realizing it was nearly one, and he was starving. Unfortunately, they didn't sell food in the exhibit hall, so he'd have to go to the adjoining hotel or find somewhere to eat on the street.

But he'd come back, stay to the end of the day and finish checking out the booths to see which ones he should revisit tomorrow. The day after, he'd be giving his presentation. Day Four was his meeting with Holstrom, and he hoped, a big celebration when he was awarded the contract.

For now, his hunger needed to be dealt with. Why he hadn't stashed a couple of protein bars in his pocket was beyond him. Especially considering the variety of bars Sam had stocked in the pantry.

Thinking about the apartment made him think of Kensey. Where had she gone last night, looking so fierce and so sexy he had forbidden himself from thinking about her during conference hours?

He quickly pulled himself back to the most pressing order of business…which was what? Yeah, right. *Food.*

Come to think of it, he needed to try some of the new kinds of nutritional substitutes being sampled in booths at the other end of the building. And not just because right now he could eat the hindquarters of a jackass. He wanted the best for the people he hired. Sometimes overlooking something small could make or break a mission. Like food, water, warmth—

"Oh, hey."

He knew that voice. And that body. Goddamn, why'd he have to run into her? "Do you know how many people are at this conference?" he asked, turning toward Kensey.

She looked surprised. "No. How many?"

"I have no idea," he said. "A lot. And we run into each other?"

She started laughing. "I'm not following you, Logan. I give you my word."

"Which is just what someone who was following me would say."

"Tell me you're joking."

He let his grin take over. "Yeah, I'm kidding. Hey, have you had lunch? I'm trying to make my way out of here to grab something."

She shook her head, making her hair swish over her shoulders. She wasn't wearing it the way she had last night. But then she wasn't wearing that dress, either. Damn thing had kept him up half the night. Thank God he hadn't seen her in it when he was fifteen. He'd have OD'd from masturbating so much. Being thirty-three had its upside.

"I've got a thing," she said. "But I'll be home this evening. What about dinner?"

That was so much better. He smiled as if he'd won a medal before calming his shit down to something a grown man would wear. "Sounds great. What time? Seven? Eight?"

She seemed to be thinking it over, which gave him a chance to look down. Mistake. Man, she was hot. Her blue-gray T-shirt was just tight enough, and the neckline was wide enough for him to become really familiar with some of her enticing secondary parts. Like the ridges of her collarbones, the toned slope of her shoulder…

And her pants… On a guy he'd call them cargo pants, but on her, they became a shrine to her curvy shape. They hugged her thighs, then went straight down to her blue-gray high heels. The middle section was covered by a very wide pinkish belt that sat squarely on her right hip then pointed south.

He couldn't wait until she turned around, because that T-shirt was tucked in. He'd have a perfect view of what had to be a damn fine behind.

"How's your afternoon?" she asked.

"You mean, now?"

"I'm just trying to figure out dinner. Either 7:00 or 8:00 would work for me, but if you have a full afternoon we can—"

"Nope. I'm tied up until 6:30. After that I'm free and clear for the night."

"Perfect," she said, and so was her smile. "How about we shoot for 7:30?"

"Great. At the apartment, right?"

"Right." She was giving him a funny look. Had he missed something? Or was he that stupidly obvious? "See you later," she said and turned around.

Even in the terrible lighting of the convention hall, her behind looked world-class. But it wasn't just her butt. The shirt's neckline dropped down in the back. Low enough for him to see that she wasn't wearing a bra.

"You have got to be kidding me."

The second Logan heard the familiar voice he shut his eyes and silently willed Kensey to leave. Now. Run.

"If it ain't Captain McBabe!"

Slowly, Logan opened his eyes. Shit. Sergeant Allan Rucker, the self-designated "Ruckster," was coming toward him, and the beautiful, incredible Kensey Unknown Last Name was turning around.

Perfect.

"Dude," Allan said. "I shoulda known I'd see you here. You end up being a spy like I said? I told you. Remember? Way back." He gripped Logan's arms and pulled him into a hug that hurt in so many ways.

Technically, he could have gotten out of it. But he wasn't about to do that. Not in front of Kensey. Not in public. "Ruckster" meant well and he'd been a good soldier back in the army. "How are you, Allan?"

"A-OK, Captain. Working for ADT in residential security. You know, doing my thing right here in Boston. Shit. I haven't seen you for, what's it been, eight years?"

"About that." He nodded, saddened by how much Allan had aged. His old acquaintance had a gut on him, and his breath smelled like beer. But he was here, so he was making it.

"You doing okay?"

"Fine."

"Good." Allan's restless gaze swept the perimeter. "Listen, Captain, I've gotta spin, but you know how to find me. Hell, you could find anybody, couldn't you?" The big guy went for a handshake, blessedly, and then that part of Logan's past disappeared again.

He didn't want to look to see if Kensey was still there.

"Captain McBabe?"

Damn it. "Yep," he said. "It's because I'm dashing and suave."

"Huh," Kensey said. Then she just looked at him for a

while. Finally, a second before he was going to break the silence, she said, "See you later."

He would. See her later. At least now he wouldn't have any trouble with rogue erections. All he had to do was imagine her calling him McBabe again.

KENSEY CLOSED THE fridge door and decided right then that she'd let Logan choose whether they ate in or went out for dinner. Either way, she wasn't going to be cooking. Now that she'd inventoried the refrigerator and seen some of the recipes Sam had left at the apartment, she understood the reason for the list of names she'd found in a drawer. With twenty-four hours' notice, guests could hire a professional chef to come in and cook for them. She got the appeal.

Even better, once she finished the pint of amazing Toscanini's pistachio ice cream she'd found in the freezer, she would be able to order another carton for delivery the next day. She might even tell Logan about it, instead of hiding the ice cream under a big bag of frozen blueberries.

In the past hour she'd learned a lot about the perks and gadgets that came with the apartment. The place was incredible. Although, she liked her own apartment an awful lot. Thanks to her father's guilt money, she owned a two-bedroom co-op in Chelsea that had become her sanctuary in New York.

She might not have an original Modigliani at her place, but she had a number of exquisite reproductions, which could fool even a regular museum visitor. Her bed was almost as nice as the one here, though not as big. But queen-size was fine for her.

All in all, she was very lucky, if one didn't count the fact that her estranged father could be caught and sent to prison unless she could prove someone else had stolen the ten-million-dollar painting he was suspected of taking. Or someone could out him as the Houdini Burglar, which would be so much worse.

She exhaled. Yeah, if one didn't count that.

Her thoughts shot to the blue box of mac and cheese she'd spotted in the pantry. If she'd had time before making the call to Neil, she would've been tempted to make herself a big bowl of comfort. Just to take the edge off her nervous energy.

Kensey checked her watch as she put her iPod and speakers on the mantel above the fireplace. Even though she'd had plenty to do since returning to the apartment, her mind hadn't truly left the exhibition hall.

It wasn't as if she'd expected Holstrom to hang out in his giant booth all day. Why would he? The exhibit was the equivalent of the kids' table for someone like him. But she'd lingered nearby, on the off chance she'd see him, or at least overhear something useful. Which, ultimately, she had. But not before she'd learned more than she ever cared to know about the large array of guns being hawked. Weapons were not of much interest to an art curator. Maybe a budding burglar...

She closed her eyes as doubt hit like a sudden storm.

She knew art. But she'd never actually planned on turning into *Lara Croft, Missing Masterpiece Hunter.* Okay maybe it sounded exciting. But still, she wasn't a burglar. Relieved that Holstrom was busy tonight at some big dinner so that she didn't have to find a way to bump into him, she turned back to her iPod and checked her selected music, for after her call.

Neil's meeting should be over by now, although if he ran late, that would be fine. As long as they were done in an hour, so she'd have time for yoga and a shower before Logan arrived.

After pouring herself a glass of water, she sat on the ultrasoft leather couch. "Call Neil Patterson." The monitor popped up on the wall. There was no connection yet, but he'd see she was waiting.

Closing her eyes, she did some deep breathing to get herself settled. The whole day she'd felt as if a giant clock was ticking, the window for her to actually pull her father's ass out of the fire dwindling by the second. Obsessively checking online for news of his possible capture hadn't helped. It was a ridiculous waste of time since she knew Neil would keep her informed.

Holstrom hadn't called her. Not yet. Not even to make plans for another night when he wasn't booked. It made sense. He was the type of man who needed to make it perfectly clear that things ran on his schedule, or they didn't run at all.

"You look comfortable."

She opened her eyes, startled at her boss's voice. "It's easy to look comfortable in this apartment. My God. You have to stay here. It's amazing."

"I'm aware."

She smiled at herself. "Of course you are."

"But I imagine being there for the experience is very different from looking at schematics and plans." His gaze moved from her to her surroundings. "That isn't your room. Are you sure we shouldn't talk somewhere more private?"

"Logan won't be back until after 6:30. I made sure," she said, feeling anxious. But if he had bad news, Neil would have said so already. "I was able to get into the party last night. A lot of interesting people were there. I can honestly say if that room had been blown up, maps would have to be rewritten. Not to mention the financial chaos that would ensue across the globe."

"So a typical Holstrom party, then."

She smiled. "I did get him to take my number. He

asked if I'd be amenable to drinks or dinner and I made sure he understood I was very open to seeing him again."

"He'll call. He's probably been checking out your background."

"Well, he sure won't find anything we don't want him to find. Your friend Sam is amazingly gifted at manipulating a person's digital presence. I almost believed some of the tweaks she made to my background."

"Yes, she does great work."

Kensey took another quick sip of water to soothe her dry mouth. It was nerves, of course, but she wished it would stop. When she put the glass down, she said, "Is there anything new?"

Neil leaned back in his leather chair. He was still in Tarrytown. It was hard to believe all that had happened in the past thirty hours.

"We haven't learned much," he said. "We know that Detective Brown hasn't found your father. In fact, I don't think he knows where to start."

"We?"

"I have a man on this. Your father didn't leave any trail. They may not find him. Ever."

Oddly, she didn't feel as relieved as she should. The little girl in her wanted to see him. Not in handcuffs, certainly, but if he disappeared forever... She shook her head at herself, then remembered Neil could see her.

Straightening, she said, "In the little digging I was able to do, I found out that Seymour has sold off some of his art collection. No major pieces, but enough to make me think he might be in some financial trouble."

Neil nodded. "He's dug himself a deep pit. He might even be in bed with some money lenders—the kind who don't threaten with lawsuits. Whatever he's done, he's nervous. My friend thinks Seymour will be the one to crack, and I'm inclined to agree. If he doesn't have a full payout from Lloyd's of London, he could lose his estate. And then there's Brown. If he's involved, he might be desperate enough to do something stupid. Before it was about ego. The longer this plays out, the more he has at stake than just losing his pension."

"You've been busy." Kensey shook her head. "I'm guessing you hired your 'friend' the minute I walked out of your office?"

"Phil's good at what he does."

"I can't tell you how grateful I am. I know your schedule better than you do, and you don't have time for this."

"I'm not actually the one doing the legwork, Kensey." He leaned forward, put his arms on his desk and looked right into the eye of his computer lens. "We're going to throw everything we've got at this problem. Holstrom might not have the Degas. And to be honest, finding the connection between Seymour and Brown and proving they conspired is the best way to help your father."

"Thank you," she managed. She wasn't good at this part. Saying things that mattered. Neil was more like a father to her than her own. He was an unconditional friend and mentor, and every time she saw that in action, she was floored.

"Don't tell me you wouldn't do the same if the roles were reversed."

She nodded, doing her best not to put up the controlled mask she wore whenever she was uncomfortable. "I'll keep moving forward out here. If Holstrom doesn't call by tomorrow, I'll give him another reminder."

"Let's hope we have a break on this end and you can leave Boston without ever seeing the bastard again."

What Kensey wouldn't give for that outcome. "One more thing. I'm curious. Do you know much about Logan McCabe? Other than he's an old friend of Sam's and that he's ex-military. There's shockingly little about him that comes up in a traditional search."

"No, I don't. Sam has never said, but I'm pretty sure he wasn't just in special operations. I think he was in black ops. That means he's smart as hell, cagey and I wouldn't want to mess with him."

"Black ops? That's CIA stuff, right?"

"I think so, yes. But again, Sam hasn't said. Either she doesn't know, or she's not allowed to say."

Kensey thought about Logan and his Pliny the Elder beer. How he'd looked at her when he'd seen her in her warrior dress. His easy smile. He was fit as hell, but lots of men were. But black ops, though? That put him in a very special league.

She smiled. "Okay. So, I don't need to worry about him."

"I never said that."

Her cheery facade vanished. "Well, that's helpful. Should I be worried?"

"No. Just careful." Neil frowned. "Is he giving you trouble?"

"No. It's just unsettling sharing the place with a stranger."

"I know," he said, using his professor voice. "Remember, you're not alone in this. So don't push Holstrom too far. He's a tricky prick." Neil leaned back. "Tell you the truth, I feel better knowing you have someone like McCabe around."

Kensey wasn't sure she agreed or wanted to think about what that meant regarding the risk she was taking, so she just nodded.

"Unless something breaks tonight, I'll speak to you tomorrow."

Long after they'd disconnected, she sat staring at the blank gray wall.

5

Unsurprisingly exhausted, Logan put his key in the door, looking forward to a quick shower then dinner with Kensey.

He didn't give a damn about what was on the menu. He'd eaten more army rations than he cared to think about. All he wanted was to talk to Kensey. Get to know her better. Then have a lot of sex.

Music met him with a bang. Hard rock, served very loud. Was she nuts?

He headed straight into the living room.

Shit.

There she was. Wearing really tiny black yoga shorts. And a white tank top, which looked a great deal like the undershirts in his dresser drawer. They looked much better on her.

She was on a yoga mat, doing a handstand with her legs curled round over her head so that her feet touched her forehead.

The *scorpion* was a bitch of a pose. Especially for men. He knew. He'd used yoga a lot during his deployments and kept up with it at home. Keeping limber was one of the first truly valuable lessons he'd learned in self-defense.

But he'd never listened to AC/DC while trying to find his spiritual center.

Of course, he was mesmerized. By her perfect form, her perfect body. She couldn't see him from this angle, and he didn't move, afraid to startle her lest she hurt herself. But mostly, he was just in awe. No training at all, she'd said. What a load. She was in better shape than some Navy SEALs he knew.

As he watched, she raised her legs into a regular handstand and did a few elbow dips. Then, boom, the music changed to typical yoga crap. A few seconds later, she shifted so that she was balancing the weight of her body entirely on one hand. A single-handed handstand. Every part of her body was stunning, her balance superb and she could call him McBabe every other minute, it wouldn't stop him from getting hard.

"Hello?" she said, still on just the one hand and unable to look his way.

"Just me. Sorry. Didn't mean to disturb you."

"No problem."

"I'll leave you to it, then."

"Wait."

He knew she couldn't see him, yet she had sensed someone was standing there and had stayed completely cool. Just like yesterday when she'd been wearing nothing but a towel. Interesting. "Yeah?"

"Are you always early? I mean, is it a thing? A little OCD maybe?"

"No. In fact, I only started doing it to annoy you."

"Ah," she said, still on the one damn hand. The way her muscles shifted to keep her balance was like an intricate ballet. "Thought so."

"Change of subject, while you're in a conversational mood. Think you could teach me that?"

"Sure. Give me about ten years, and voilà—you'll be a yoga master."

"Ten years. Ha. I get it. That's a joke." *Okay, smartass. Game on.* "No seriously. How about that thing you were doing a minute ago?"

"The scorpion?"

"Yeah."

"Maybe. Can you do a handstand?"

"I'm ex-military. I can do fifty before breakfast."

"I'm pretty sure that's called cheerleading, but, hey, to each his own."

"Again. Funny. Anyway, I'll wait until you're done. Wouldn't want you to hurt yourself and blame me."

She transitioned into a double-handed handstand, then lowered herself into a sitting position in one of the most graceful moves he'd ever seen. "Take off your shoes," she said.

He didn't think twice about it, just took 'em off where he stood.

"Do you want to change first?"

"Damn. I forgot to pack my yoga clothes."

"Okay." A faint smile tugged at her lips. Oh, yeah... she was gonna put him through the wringer. "Let me see your handstand."

Something occurred to him that he should've considered before he'd opened his mouth. He was a little hard and that was going to make things difficult. "You know what? I interrupted your routine, which was really thoughtless, so I'll just—"

"Why McBabe, you surprise me."

Logan sighed. At least his cock was calming down. "You're going to use that all the time, aren't you?"

"Probably. Just to annoy you." She got to her feet. Not like regular humans did. Like goddesses rose from those giant lily pads. "I can go get a towel and wipe down my mat if you're afraid of girl cooties."

"I think I can handle it," he said and met the challenge in her eyes with one of his own.

Her gaze held for a moment, and then she was all business. "Okay, come on over."

He walked to the middle of the living room, right in front of the fireplace. The sound of some hippie playing the flute filled the space, but the walls weren't in tune. They had been when AC/DC had nearly broken his eardrums. Now they'd turned to a brick red and pulsed like a heartbeat.

"Put one foot in front of the other," she said. "Lift your back leg up and raise your arms straight out in front of you so your body forms a T."

He obeyed and made no further comment. But she was close. Next to him, walking around him, and he could smell her. Her scent was so utterly feminine it made him a little shaky.

"Steady," she said, her shoulder briefly brushing his arm. "Now put your leg down and press your palms on the ground with arms straight. Gently rock forward and back. Inhale forward, exhale back until you feel steady enough to lift one leg off the ground. There you go."

She touched his arm again. Her palm was soft and warm against his skin, and the feel of it momentarily threw him off.

He breathed in, exhaled slowly, then not only got one leg up, but two. And he started arching them backward.

She moved her hand to his thigh. To help guide him. But it was unexpected.

He fell. Hard.

"Logan." She was on her knees in two seconds. "Are you okay? Oh, God." She touched his chest, quickly drew back her hand. "Where does it hurt?"

"I'm fine."

"Nothing broken?" She probed his arm with feather-light fingertips, her green eyes dark with concern.

He knew he should reassure her that he was okay but he didn't want her to stop touching him. Or to move away. He could feel her breath on his jaw, her body heat warming his skin. All he wanted to do was kiss her. "Logan?"

"I'm okay."

"Promise?" Her lips parted as they almost met his. They shared a breath, back and forth.

He had a second to wish he'd shaved before he kissed her, but in that moment he saw uncertainty flicker in her eyes. So he did a quick kick up. From horizontal to vertical in the fastest way he knew how.

Kensey was still on the floor, but he could see her stunned expression. Which shifted to pissed off. Whether it was because he'd stopped the kiss or she thought that he'd played her, he couldn't tell.

He was pretty sure he'd find out.

"COME ON," LOGAN SAID, extending a hand to her, as if she needed help to stand. "You know I'm ex-military."

After batting him away, she got to her feet. "Yeah, because everyone in the military is completely fit and knows how to do kick ups."

He shrugged. "You got me there."

"I think you're the one who got me," she muttered, and thought about stepping back. They were standing awfully close. But the hell with that. She wouldn't be the one to chicken out. He'd been about to kiss her. She hadn't gotten that part wrong. So what happened?

"I'm sorry," he said, the laugh lines crinkling at the corners of his eyes contradicting his words. "I think my ego needed a boost after seeing what you can do. Talk about a yoga master."

"I'm not that special. I've been doing it for a long time."

He shook his head as he leaned in her direction. "I've been cooking for a long time. Doesn't make me a chef. You had to work damn hard to do that."

"When I'm not going to fancy conferences, I work with incredibly expensive art. I need to be ready for anything."

"Anything?"

Still smarting from his slick move, she said, "So, you learned that in the military, huh? Was that special ops?" She hadn't thrown him off-balance as she'd hoped. "Or was it black ops?"

Bingo.

He didn't even blink. In fact, his expression hardly changed. Yet he managed to make her wish with all her heart she could take back the stupid taunt. His guard had gone up as swiftly as the words had fallen from her lips. She'd never seen anything like it. The change in him had a little to do with his eyes, and some to do with his posture, but it was much more than that.

She was looking at the soldier. Neil was right. Logan wasn't a man to be messed with.

He'd bested her in a stupid contest that had no meaning, and she'd made everything worse by throwing down the gauntlet. Damn it, if he thought she'd been poking around his background, he could start poking back. Someone like him might have the resources to find out about her father.

She had to do something. And not just because the tense silence was doing a number on her.

"I was nervous about sharing the place with a strange man," she said, offering him a smile and her most relaxed voice. "So Sam told me you'd been in special ops, and I figured it was okay that I knew or she wouldn't have said anything." It wasn't completely accurate, what she'd said.

Neil had been the one to tell her about special ops, but she wanted Logan to relax so they could get off this topic.

Kensey touched his muscled arm and knew she'd screwed up badly when he didn't react to her touch as he had before. "I'm sorry if I upset you. Today I heard a lot of reps in the gun booths bragging about how special-ops soldiers use their brand. I didn't think it was a secret. Although, yeah, there had been a lot of talk about the ID of SEAL Team Six, so…"

"It's not a secret," Logan said just as she'd given up hope that he'd ever speak to her again. "I use my experience to drum up business. And I make it known that I hire other special-ops vets. No big deal." He stepped back, effectively dislodging her hand from his arm. "So, what's for dinner?"

"Oh, about that…" She sighed, glad to change the subject. Not that she thought this was over. This man staring at her was a different Logan. Most people probably wouldn't notice the slight edginess to his smile. But she was good at reading people. Something else she'd learned from her father. And dammit, if she wanted to prove his innocence, she had to stop baiting Logan and focus on why she was there. "I'm not cooking. We can go out for dinner, or order something to be delivered. Either way, my treat."

"Ah, man. I was looking forward to a home-cooked meal."

"Trust me, there is nothing in that fridge that will resemble your idea of home cooking."

"Too fancy for you?" Logan's grin made him look more like himself. Or at least more like the Logan he'd wanted her to see from the beginning. She needed to remember he had that ability. She had the same gift.

"It all comes with directions," he said, his voice easy and gently teasing. "I actually recognized some of it."

"Good." Moving away from him caused a bit of a tug in her chest. But this was for the best. She had one job here in Boston. One. As appealing as he was, Logan wasn't it. "Put your cooking where your mouth is. But make it snappy because I'm starving. Also, I need to shower and change clothes, so why don't—"

He grabbed her hand and pulled her toward the kitchen. "You look great. What was the food that made you throw in the towel?"

She raised both eyebrows.

"What?"

"You had to bring up the towel?"

He choked out a laugh. "I didn't even think— But now that you mention it…"

She turned away from the arousal darkening his eyes and opened the freezer door. That glimpse of Logan's dangerous side had turned her on but she couldn't let herself go in that direction. The frigid air did little to cool her down but the overwhelming amount of food inside somewhat distracted her. In her freezer, she had an ice maker, a roasting chicken and ice cream in a few different flavors. That was it. "That one." She pointed to a white package.

"Duck rillettes?" Logan frowned. "What is that?"

"I have no idea. Do ducks really have a part on them that are called *rillettes*?"

Logan shook his head and moved closer so he could see better. So that they were touching. Again. Only this time, she pressed against his shoulder and seconds later, he pressed against her hip. He felt warm where he touched her. Her bare thighs rubbed against his jeans, and the frigid air made her nipples harden.

She wondered if the air had the same effect on him. She couldn't see his nipples through his shirt, and freezing air wasn't going to harden anything down south.

He turned over the package, looking as if he was settling in for the evening. Maybe he really did want that home-cooked meal.

Or maybe this was a way to relax her defenses. A clever way for him to find out what she knew about him.

Then again, he might be wondering the same thing about her. And he wouldn't be wrong. Not completely. She had been trying to find out more about him. Was he a safe haven or a rocky shoal? It would be stupid to think of him as either. To think of him at all.

The thought made her feel ridiculously sad.

"According to this," he said, "it's duck that's been smoked and shredded with duck fat, salt and pepper, and meant to be slathered over stuff. And eaten with a side of pickles."

It didn't appeal to her in the least. Gourmet it might be, but she'd never been a foodie, and that wasn't going to change now. "We're ordering out."

They were still touching. He had to lean sideways to look at her. "You're giving up that easily?"

"Yep." She closed the freezer door and saw his gaze drop to her chest. Right where her nipples poked the fabric of her tank top. "There are menus from a bunch of places that deliver," she said. "Thai, Mexican, deli, Indian." She moved to the pantry and grabbed the stack of menus from a pouch on the inside of the door. "Unless you'd rather go out. Going out is fine." Probably better, now that she thought about it.

The effort it took for him to look her in the eyes and not ogle her breasts made her bite back a laugh.

"No, let's stay in." He got a beer out of the fridge and popped the can open.

"You sure? Boston has some great restaurants."

"I'm sure it does. But going out? Not crazy about the idea." Angled away from her, he took a gulp. Then wiped his mouth. "Sorry. You want one?"

She shook her head and did her own shifting to hide the front of her tank. "We should place an order, then shower while we wait for the food."

He glanced at her, one brow lifted.

"I meant...separately. Of course."

Logan shrugged, looking as if he disagreed. About which part, though? "If you insist," he said, finally turning toward her.

Well, damn if she hadn't been wrong about the effects of an open freezer on a man's ability to get hard.

"Tell you what," he said, and she forced her gaze up to his face. "You order something while I make a quick call. Okay?"

She nodded, then jerked her gaze up again. "Yes. Fine. Go."

He couldn't seem to leave fast enough.

She watched him until he turned the corner, and steadied herself against the nearest countertop. Truth was, the train had left the station. For both of them. Heading in only one direction. She just hoped they weren't in for an epic wreck.

"CALL SAM."

He only had to wait a few seconds for her to pop up on the wall. But then she told him to hang on. He immediately thought about Kensey. Not the part where he wanted to pull her into his bed and not let her go till morning. He wanted to know why she'd asked him about black ops.

People didn't just think of black ops. Which meant she knew something about him, but what? No regular search engine would connect him with anything on the CIA side. And the only other person who knew was Lisa. So, what the hell? Besides, why would anyone start to dig? He could understand Holstrom trying to find out whatever he could, but why would Kensey bother?

He turned the problem around and around, unable to come up with anything that made sense.

"Hey, what's up, Logan?" Sam was all dressed up, which wasn't the norm for her. She usually wore the computer geek special: jeans and a T-shirt.

"You going somewhere?"

"Yep. To a party. Where I intend to get drunk."

"Well, good for you. That'll show 'em."

Sam rolled her eyes. "You called?"

"Did you ever talk to Kensey about me working in special operations?"

Sam shrugged. "Maybe. Although I think I only said military, but I can't swear to that."

"What about black ops?" He couldn't imagine Sam saying anything like that. She didn't know, but she had helped him blur his background, and she was too smart not to put two and two together.

"You mean did I— No. Why would I?"

"Okay. Never mind. I was just checking."

"I'm pretty sure she's who she claims to be, if that's what's got you worried."

"I'm being overcautious."

"More like paranoid."

"Yeah, yeah. Listen. Would you turn off whatever the hell program it is that's making me so damn horny? I mean I like the whole scent and colors thing, but—"

Sam burst out laughing. Really laughing.

"I'm serious."

When Sam caught her breath she said, "I don't have any such program. That's all you."

"Really?"

She wiped the bottoms of her eyes. "Damn you, Logan. I never wear makeup and now you have to make me…" She started laughing again. "Just try not to break anything in your rush to—"

He hung up. Adjusted himself in his jeans, then went to the kitchen. Kensey was bent over a drawer, and he hoped that she wouldn't stand up any time soon. But she did. Then she went for an even lower drawer. He crossed his arms over his chest and enjoyed the view.

When she finally turned around she nearly jumped out of her skin. "Holy…how long have you been standing there?"

"Two drawers worth. What are you looking for?"

She paused, looking like a cornered animal. "The take-out menus—"

He nodded to the stack on the counter. "You already have them."

"Fine." Her cheeks were flushed, her eyes dilated. "I was looking for the manual."

"For the apartment?" he asked, guessing she had the same problem as him.

When she couldn't stop her gaze from checking his fly, and her hips moved in a way that had everything to do with sex, he crossed the distance between them and pulled her into the kiss he'd been holding on to from the moment he'd seen her.

She kissed him back. Deep and real and just messy enough to match the urgency that was coiling inside him like a rattler. It was everything he'd wanted, and as an added bonus, he'd just discovered that Ms. Cool wasn't a very good liar.

6

"Wait," she said a split second before he crushed her mouth with his. She could feel his desperation, in the way he pulled her against him. Made her feel what she'd done to him.

In return, she gave as good as she got, thrusting into his hot mouth for every pulse of his erection against her low belly. Logan's hand moved under her tank top and slid around to her back. Then he stroked her, moaning as he reached all the way to her neck before sliding down again.

Not that he missed a trick with his mouth. He kept up the barrage of thrusts and parries until she was breathless. The way her nipples hardened had nothing to do with the cold.

That hand, that wicked hand under her top moved to her front, and his moan when he cupped her flesh curled her toes. Seconds later, while she was still reveling in the feel of his large, rough hand, he pulled back. Before she could even show her displeasure, her tank was over her head and thrown somewhere in the real world.

In this world, Logan smiled as he bent down to suck on the nipple that had been hoping for more action.

As his thumb twirled one bud, he teased the other with

a gentle rasp of teeth, then suction, then some masterful flicking that made her feel as if she might have already died and gone to heaven.

Letting go of him, she pulled on his dark blue button-down until the shirt was up under his pits, but she couldn't do anything with it there. In fact, she couldn't do anything but flail behind her until she found the countertop to balance herself as he switched nipples, evidently going for the gold.

Damn what he could do with his tongue. Holy crap. The flicking. The flicking! Just the very tip made her insane. Then, like a dragonfly, he moved from tip to tip, back and forth.

Finally, she gripped his shoulders and pulled him up until she could look him in the eyes. "Bedroom. Now."

He seemed dazed. Completely unaware of how ridiculous he looked with his shirt bunched up so high he couldn't put his arms down. She even pointed out the problem, but he just shrugged, and took her by the hand down the hallway to his bedroom.

She laughed the whole way.

He stopped at the bed, pulled down his shirt only to unbutton it in record time, and swiftly yanked down the covers.

God bless America, he was built like...like the men in her dreams. They all had his kind of body—muscled, but not misshapen, a subtle six pack, just enough hair that she could play with it during the cooldown after and a trim waist that led to a very impressive erection.

"This is the part where you take off your shorts. Unless you'd like me to—"

They hit the floor before he could finish.

He smiled. The kind of smile that changed his face. Made him look younger. Sexy as all get-out. "You're gorgeous," he said. The rough voice was new. Also sexy. "When you wore that dress last night? I…haven't gotten over that yet."

With a move she hadn't expected, he lifted her bridal style, then laid her on the bed. Caveman Logan with that smoky voice? Different. A few miles more than good. It was as if she'd been sent back in time, to an age where her stomach was all butterflies and giggles were going to erupt if she didn't do something soon.

He lifted her knees until her feet were flat on the mattress, her head resting on a pillow, and she waited breathlessly for what came next.

To say this wasn't her typical style was a huge understatement. A part of her wanted to take the reigns from Logan and show him a thing or two, but that urge was overpowered by a feeling of freedom she hadn't experienced in years.

"Lift," he said, holding a pillow down by her butt. She did.

Perhaps she should tell him that while cunnilingus was great and all, she wasn't all that into foreplay. But he seemed so intent.

He looked down at her, his eyes ablaze with desire. God, his nostrils flared. "Last night I wanted to stop you," he said with that gravelly voice. "Make you stay." He got on the bed and maneuvered himself neatly between her thighs. "Which is crazy, because I don't usually react so…viscerally."

Then he dropped to his hands and knees. His breath painted the insides of her thighs. She held perfectly still as he leaned in and kissed her gently, on her inner thigh, and then bit her.

Not hard. Just a little nip that made her start. Excited her. Even more exciting was when he licked the delicate skin where her thigh ended.

How had she not known that crease where her leg met her torso was an erogenous zone? It so was. At least when he licked her there, then blew warm air on the strip. Instead of reaching out and grabbing on to his hair, she gripped the bottom sheet.

He'd placed her so well she didn't have to move at all to watch him. The way he looked—his need so raw—made her pulse climb through the roof. It was all there in the tiny smile that hadn't gone away, even when he'd been arranging the pillows. In the black of his pupils, his lids at half-mast as his body prepared for pleasure.

A moment later, he was down too low for her to see his eyes. But she felt him at her already parted lips. He spread them and brushed his thumbs up and down. "So soft," he whispered.

Before she could answer, two fingers went inside her. Deep.

She gasped and arched, ready for far more than fingers.

He laughed, a low chuckle that made her smile in return.

"I wish you could feel this the way I feel it," he said. "I don't think it's possible, though. Sad, because I'm convinced there's nothing in the world softer than a woman. And now I've just learned that not all women feel as good as you."

She blushed. Why, she had no idea. It was a sweetly odd compliment. Something he couldn't have gotten away with if he'd been younger. But the man was in his thirties, and he'd lived a great deal of life in those years. He wouldn't bother with empty compliments.

"Christ," he said, and a second later his tongue joined the party. Her back arched again and she might have ripped the sheet, but she didn't give a damn because he was using his mad tongue skills where it counted.

No more gentle breaths and languid kisses. This was a full-on assault. The way he pushed his fingers inside her with exactly the right pressure to feel amazing while at the same time making her desperate for more? Jesus.

That tongue. She'd thought he'd been clever with her nipples, but he treated her to a range of sensations that stole her breath away, only to steal it again and again.

Flicks with the tip; suction with his lips in a perfect circle around her clit; licking with the widest part of his tongue, a soft, soft rasp, barely there and making her ache for it. All the while he was thrusting inside her, fast then slow, then fast again until she was crying out like someone in a porno. Wake-the-neighbors loud. When she opened her eyes she realized she'd wrapped her legs around his head. No recollection of doing so at all.

Suffocation by thighs didn't make him slow down at all. He kept on driving her crazy. There it was, deep down in her belly, the spark of what was sure to be an epic orgasm.

"Wait," she said, unable to tell if he'd even heard her. "Wait, I'm going to come."

Something happened down there, with his mouth against her and his fingers becoming still. "Are you laughing at me?" Damn, now her voice was wrecked. "Stop. I'm serious."

Their eyes met, and she almost came from that alone. He looked like what orgasms felt like. "I'll stop if you want," he said, "but there's no way you're not coming more than once tonight."

"Okay," she said. Then let out the air she'd been holding in one big huff. "Go for it."

That quirk, that one-sided grin that made it look like he had all the answers. She was a sucker for that, which was—

Holy shit, he'd brought out the big guns. Three fingers. Hard. Hard. Hard. Her body writhing as he sucked on her clit until the low thrum inside her became a crash, her whole body coming so hard she jackknifed and nearly clipped his chin.

Oxygen. She needed a lot of it. Especially when every aftershock made her gasp, made her twitch and constrict. Great gulps of air left her mouth dry. She needed something to suck on.

That made her laugh because, no. All the energy molecules in her body were resting.

Nope, wrong. There was another aftershock: a doozy.

Logan walked back to the bed, and it startled her to realize she hadn't noticed that he'd left. It was clear that he hadn't jacked off in the bathroom, which she wouldn't have blamed him for. She'd been on Planet Pleasure and hadn't given a thought to taking care of him.

Until now. He had a great-looking cock. Big but not intimidating, and he had to be aching for release.

Suddenly, she wasn't quite as wasted as she'd been. He sat below her between her legs saying something about a condom, which was good. Then he spread himself over her like a duvet. The molecules weren't just up, they were raring to go.

LOGAN HAD MADE sure the condom was on well before he spread out, balancing on his bent arms as they kissed. It turned him on that she could taste herself on his tongue. The noise she made as they rubbed themselves together from knee to chest. Evidently, she'd recovered.

He rubbed his cock on the bottom sheet as he kissed her.

It wasn't cutting it. Not the kiss, the other——

Screw it. They could kiss later.

Balancing his weight on his left side, he slid his free arm down between them ready to take her to the next level.

A moment later, he was flat on his back and she was grinning. "I wasn't expecting that."

"If you had, it would have spoiled all the fun."

Fun. He doubted it. Somebody had control issues. Which he understood completely. It seemed like a worthy endeavor, when to give in and when to take charge. Kensey was challenging. He liked it.

She mounted him just above where he desperately wanted her.

He groaned, anticipating the ride ahead. He was in a good position to thrust up, but with her on top, it would be more difficult to make her come again.

He couldn't remember a time he'd been harder. His little breather had helped, though. Not a lot, but still. It only felt as if he was going to die if she didn't do something soon. The longer she waited, the more likely he'd come at the first slide inside her.

Her hand slipped between them, but she didn't touch his cock. He couldn't tell what she was doing although she did it for a hell of a long time. She even bent forward, bringing her lips close enough to breathe with him. He tried to make it more interesting, but she ducked away.

"Okay, what is this? Are you trying to kill me?"

"No," she said, with so much conviction he knew it was a flat-out lie. "I want to make you feel good."

"Do I get to vote on how?"

She shook her head, and her hair brushed against his chest so close to his nipples he nearly cried. And his nipples weren't even that sensitive.

A moment that lasted a week later, and she was kind of riding him, but he wasn't inside her. Close though.

Son of a bitch, she had him rubbing between her cheeks.

He grabbed on to her hips, because he was pretty sure he was going to stroke out on this. This new sensation.

It wasn't penetrative, but the idea of what she'd done to slick up, to make it this smooth…

His hips jerked up, but Kensey wasn't having any of that. She held him right where she wanted him.

As much as he liked this, he was going to have to take matters into his own hands pretty damn soon. Did she think for a minute that he couldn't flip her right back—

Holy shit, holy… She slid onto his erection, all the way, then rose again. Until he wasn't inside her. But not for long.

His moan had just awakened anyone who'd fallen asleep after Kensey's impressive performance.

It was nothing short of amazing. The tension in him was enough to power his van for three blocks. No pattern, no rhythm. Just one type of stimulation versus another until he was a gibbering idiot.

No more. Just…

He flipped them. Didn't tease her. Just hit it hard, one thrust. Another.

She grabbed him by the head, her hands literally clutching his hair and keeping him where he was.

His top half stilled. His hips? Not even a hiccup.

Instead of the lecture he'd braced himself for, she pulled him down while she rose to meet him. Another kiss. Harder this time. Wet, sloppy and exactly right. But he couldn't hold the position much longer.

She let him go, and he managed to slip his fingers between them, finding her soft folds in seconds.

This was it. The show stopper. The part where this gorgeous woman came for the second, maybe third time in a mad race against his own skills and her responsiveness. She'd better hurry, though.

As her own quick orgasm hit, she squeezed his cock. He made a sound he'd never heard before. His hand stopped. Maybe his heart had, too, at least for a second. Stars and bolts of light danced behind his eyelids as he came.

"BREATHE," KENSEY SAID, shaking him, and she really hoped she hadn't done anything permanent to her voice. She was on the edge of hyperventilating, herself, but Logan… "You're turning funny colors. Oh. That's the walls."

He took her advice, anyway, and finally she could try to recover from her own climax. Before tonight, she'd never come more than once during sex. It hadn't bothered her. She just figured it depended on a lot of factors.

She was looking at her trembling hands when Logan kissed her. Then he launched himself over to the other side of the mattress.

Watching him move, she was caught up by the dance of muscles in his arms. Lean and mean—that was a perfect description. Then she looked at his face again. His great smile, how his eyelashes skimmed his cheeks. "Were you married?" she asked.

"Hmm? When?"

"Ever."

"No."

"Huh," she said. "That was epic, by the way." She turned onto her side to face him only to find he'd done the same thing. They were curled up next to each other, both of them smiling.

"My thoughts, exactly."

"But…"

He raised his eyebrows.

"I'm starving."

His stomach responded for him. "That means getting out of bed. Think we can call the Thai restaurant and have them deliver to the bedroom in the next ten minutes?"

"We could try. You never know. Although, I think we'll have better luck if we're not completely naked for the delivery person." She brushed his cheek with her thumb. "There's an awful lot of food in the pantry. Bet we could make something easy."

"Make? I don't have enough energy to open a box of Twinkies."

"Huh," she murmured. "I could go for Twinkies."

Smiling, he tucked a lock of hair behind her ear. "Have I told you how amazing you are?"

She kissed him. The past hour and a half had been amazing for her, too, for many reasons. Not the least being the fact that she hadn't given one thought to her father, the Degas, Holstrom, Neil or the very big mess she called her life.

7

"WE CAN STILL order Thai."

Logan shook his head. "It'll take too long."

"So eat a little something now and, o-kay. Never mind."

He'd opened the pantry door. The vast amount of food on the shelves suggested that there was a Harry Potter thing going on where the inside grew to accommodate everything put in it. It was also organized to the last inch, and part of him wanted to just go crazy putting things in the wrong places.

Kensey came up beside him. They were both wearing their apartment-issued Turkish robes. She looked much better in hers than he did in his, but she could wear any damn thing she wanted to and still make his heart beat triple time.

"If I wasn't so against the entire concept of cooking anything, I'd pull out the mac and cheese. I doubt it's a normal staple for this place. Sam understands my annoying obsession with it. She used to send me cases of the stuff when I was in the Sandbox."

"That's Iraq?"

He nodded. "It is. I had to hide my care packages before I was mobbed."

"I had to hide it as well."

"How come?"

Her lips lifted in an odd smile. "I went to a Swiss board-ing school. If I'd gotten caught with a box, I would've been expelled," she said. "But not before I was shamed in front of the entire student body."

"Hell, that's child abuse."

Kensey blinked at him. "I was kidding. They wouldn't have—"

"I meant depriving you of mac and cheese."

She bumped him with her shoulder.

"Damn Europeans." Logan stole a kiss. "What do they know about cheese?"

Her laugh lit her green eyes. When he leaned in for another kiss, she caught his jaw and redirected him to the well-stocked shelves. "Food first," she said.

"First?" He grinned. "I like the sound of that."

She just shook her head, her hair floating around her shoulders in a sexy, tousled blond cloud, a smile teasing the corners of her lips.

Boarding school didn't surprise him. In fact, maybe that was where she'd learned that cool composure. He could easily see her living in a fancy Manhattan apart-ment surrounded by priceless art. She wore minimal jew-elry, a Rolex watch and sometimes earrings. Diamond studs. He'd bet his own modest Tribeca walk-up those rocks were the real thing.

Yet she wasn't standoffish. It was easy talking to her, and the sex had been off the charts, but he shouldn't ex-pect anything. He could hope they ended up in bed again. Food first implied they might. This was just an interlude. It would have been different if they'd gotten dressed, but he was almost certain that robes meant the sex wasn't over.

"There's quinoa," she said. "That's only fifteen minutes."

"Too long."

"Pizza delivery?"

"Wait just a minute," he said, reaching for the red-and-blue box of Cap'n Crunch. "I haven't had this in years."

She laughed. "And I thought you were a big bad soldier man."

"Who's liberal about his food choices. There's also some Raisin Bran, if you're into that kind of—"

"Oh, my God. Frosted Flakes." She plowed in front of him to get the box, and when she turned around, grinning, he knew they had a special connection. At least when it came to food. And sex. The rest? He didn't need to know. They only had a few days.

She brought the milk, he found the bowls and the spoons, and they sat opposite each other at the small kitchen table.

"So," he said, halfway through his first bowl of cereal. "Boarding school, huh? Is that where they make you walk with books on your head to teach you good posture?"

Kensey lowered her spoon. "Are you joking?" she asked, staring, waiting. "Seriously. I can't tell."

"Hey, most of the time I can't figure out what's going on in that head of yours, either."

She didn't comment. Just shifted her gaze and ate another spoonful of cereal.

Well, hell, Logan wasn't looking to kill the mood. "Yes, I was joking. Where are you from? I mean, are your folks American? European?"

"My mother is French. I was born in New York. When I wasn't in school I bounced back and forth between France and Manhattan. According to Sam, you're from the city, as well."

"Yep, but not the fancy part. I live in Tribeca. My office is in Brooklyn." He could almost see the walls going up around her. So, she didn't like talking about her family. That was okay. "Is this your first security conference?"

She looked up, nodding. "I've wanted to attend for a couple of years but there always seemed to be a conflict."

"What are you looking for?"

"Fine art is a specialty, although a lot of the same kinds of security procedures are used to protect antiquities, high-end jewelry, valuable books…those sorts of things. I like keeping up with the latest tech."

"Is that the responsibility of a curator?" He poured some more Crunch, then topped up his milk. "I don't know much about fine art. Or what a curator does."

"I don't decide on the security features, but I make recommendations. A lot of what I'll be doing now that I'm a freelancer is helping private collectors protect their art. There are storage concerns, lighting…a lot goes into preserving art. I'm also in charge of moving pieces, whether it's been sold or being loaned out to a museum. For example, after I get back to New York, I'm taking a van Gogh to Vienna."

"For…?"

"A private client."

"Right," he said. "Of course. You think you'll like freelancing better than staying with one collection?"

"Not necessarily. But it does give me more freedom."

"That's worth a hell of a lot," he said.

They ate for a bit, both of them crunching their way to satiety. Logan had never had a problem with silence, generally preferred it. But something was still bothering him. "I was wondering. What made you ask about black ops?"

Kensey didn't look up right away, but he saw the blush creeping up her throat. "I guess I should stick to what I know." She shrugged and the robe slipped off her left shoulder, exposing the swell of her breast. She tugged the thick fabric back in place. "I was checking out the different booths and listening to the reps promoting their weapons collections. It was kind of funny, really. Every time they lowered their voice you knew they were going to tout their brand as being the number one choice for black ops."

Logan smiled. "And did people believe them?"

She seemed to give it some thought. "You know…I think half of them did. They seemed impressed."

"Do you carry?"

She blinked. "A gun? No," she said, shaking her head and pulling the front of her robe together. "When I escort a piece I usually have at least one armed guard with me, though, usually two."

"So, why the interest in the gun booths?"

"I'm considering buying a small pistol." She put down her spoon and narrowed her gaze. "It feels like you're grilling me. Did I blunder into something? Are you black ops?"

He watched her lean forward slightly, her eyes bright with interest and maybe excitement. If she was acting, she was doing a hell of a good job. Under the table her bare toes brushed his, and damned if that didn't send his thoughts straight to sex. Her naked. Flushed with arousal. Panting beneath him. "No, I'm not black ops."

"Oh." She leaned back. "To be honest, I'm not sure what black ops is. Or how it differs from special ops or covert ops."

"Who knows if there's any such thing as black ops. It's probably nothing but a way for Hollywood to make war and espionage look glamorous."

"You must hate that. I'm guessing any soldier who has seen combat would be offended."

"What makes you think I saw combat?" He swallowed his last mouthful and the lump that her words had brought to his throat. She'd looked so fierce in defense of him and his brothers in arms. He smiled. "Maybe I was a cook."

Kensey laughed. "I doubt your group or team, whatever you call it, would've been happy with mac and cheese and cold cereal." Tilting her head to the side, she studied him for a moment. "You don't strike me as the kind of man who would shy away from the action. So yes, I'm thinking you saw your share of combat."

That was an understatement.

Logan decided he'd overreacted to her black ops remark and relaxed. And not because she'd been ready to defend him. When her robe had slipped off her shoulder and distracted him, she hadn't used the opportunity to avoid his questions. She'd immediately covered up. Anyway, he'd been out of the field too long to be looking back at shadows. These days he was an ordinary Joe. And he was pretty sure Kensey was exactly who she claimed to be—a curator who'd attended a Swiss boarding school so she could learn all about the finer things in life.

And damn she was hot.

If he had anything to say about it, there was going to be a lot more sex tonight.

KENSEY WATCHED LOGAN watch her. She had stumbled earlier in the evening. That was putting it kindly. He had played her and she'd stupidly struck back with the unfortunate black ops mention. And now he wasn't sure if he could trust her.

"You know what?" she said. "You and any other soldier who's fought have every right to be insulted by someone trivializing military service for monetary gain. Tomorrow, if I'm near any of those weapons' booths, I'm going to point out how disrespectful they're being."

Logan laughed. "You're just trying to get me to kiss you."

"No, I'm not," she said. The thing was she meant it. She had never thought about it before, but now that she had...

"What?" He had the oddest look on his face. "Getting you to

kiss me is easy. All I'd have to do is—" Struggling to come up with something quick and clever, she waved a hand.

"Drop your robe?" The hopeful puppy dog eyes were adorable.

"No. Not what I was going to say." She reached across the table to touch his large, tanned hand. Just thinking about his rough palm cupping her bare breasts started a flutter in her tummy. "Forgive me. I shouldn't have brought up the subject at all."

"It's okay." Logan squeezed her hand. "You'd be surprised at how many people flat-out ask what it's like to fight in a war. I tell them it's like going to another planet. The same rules don't apply."

"I know you were in the army. This afternoon that man at the exhibition center called you Captain."

"I was in the regular army with him, then I went to special ops. Basically, I was an army ranger. And Delta Force."

"Really? I saw that movie with Chuck Norris a long time ago."

"That was more hype than truth."

"Of course." Kensey blushed and leaned back, moving her hand to her lap.

Logan smiled. "But yeah, it's tough to come home. I'm giving a presentation in two days about what guys face after a tour. The world you lived in was one of absolute vigilance. The fight or flight response never turns off. And then you're back in a happy suburb in Cleveland or LA and every sound is magnified, every movement suspect. It takes a lot of practice to be a civilian again. Especially for spec-ops personnel because they tend to do more than one tour. That's not to say they come home burned-out. They bring a whole lot of invaluable skills back with them."

Kensey almost asked him how many times he'd been deployed but stopped herself.

"I'm trying to get more companies to see that and hire vets. The thing they want most is to feel useful again. And hell, it's not charity. Too many people don't understand what it means to have a trained special-ops soldier on their team. My security company is still small but other than my sister, everyone is ex-military. Most of them are on-call because I don't have enough work yet, but that's slowly changing. We were involved in taking down an international sex trafficking operation last year. So we've picked up more clients."

"The bust that happened in New York?"

He nodded.

"I read about that," she said. "In the *Times*. I don't remember seeing your name, though."

"No, you wouldn't have. It doesn't matter. That kind of publicity won't get me the business I need. I'm looking at a bigger picture. My goal is to have two thousand full-time employees within five years. Maybe more. It's doable but it'll take money and connections. I'm hoping to sign on as a subcontractor with someone here who has both. I've got a lot riding on it." Logan exhaled. "Every day more and more vets are coming home to nothing. The people I hire know therapy for every employee is nonnegotiable. So everybody gets help, which is another consideration."

Kensey let what he'd said sink in for a minute. He really was one of the good guys, wasn't he? He'd already served his country, and now he wanted to help his fellow vets train and heal so they could live the civilian life, yet use the skills they'd learned through their service.

"How many did you do?" she asked, finally, unable to stop herself. "Tours, I mean."

"A lot," he said with a wry smile. "The thing is, in between deployments you don't get to go home and chill, you're in training to go on your next tour."

"I can't imagine."

"I don't know. From what I've seen so far, you'd make a great candidate for a certain type of work."

"Nope. I'm too independent. I've never been great at groups of anything."

"No Girl Scouts?"

"I only eat the cookies."

Logan sat up straight. "There's gotta be cookies in that pantry. You want to come look?"

"Nope. I've just had my sugar allotment for the day. For several days, actually."

"Come on. Don't be like that. Staying here? The best R & R ever? The cookies have to be killer." He held out his hand to her, and she couldn't say no.

Not that she gave a damn about the cookie assortment. She liked the warm, tingly feel of his palm pressed to hers. Middle school kids held hands. It wasn't a big deal, certainly nothing that should feel this incredibly intimate. Yet it did. Another oddity... She couldn't remember ever being with a man and feeling relaxed enough to let her guard down. It was easy to do with Logan. Maybe too easy.

He rooted around until he found the cookies. It was like watching a kid at Christmas. He turned to her, his expression helpless with a kind of awed joy. "Double Stuf," he said, as if he was talking about the *Mona Lisa*. "They melted into guck by the time they arrived where I was stationed. I missed them. A lot."

"Aww, that makes me not want to make fun of you."

He turned on her again, only this time so sharply she jumped. "Make fun of me, eh? I've got a good memory, Kensey whatever-your-last-name-is. I will remember this."

She was already laughing at his inability to remember her last name, but what got her... "Really? You think you can remember something for three more days? That's amazing. I should have known you were in Delta Force."

He couldn't keep a straight face, either, and it felt like heaven to just laugh like this. Over something silly and meaningless. Laughing just because it felt good. Laughing *with* someone.

With Logan.

He put the cookies on the counter, then settled his hands on her hips and smiled. She looked up into his handsome face, tilting her head back to maintain eye contact as he pulled her against him. She was tall, with or without heels, but with both of them barefooted, he seemed so much taller than she was. It was kind of nice for a change.

She lifted a palm to rest on his chest and he lowered his mouth to hers. He brushed a soft kiss across her lips, and then he adjusted the angle of his head. Just as his tongue swept past her parted lips, his hand slipped inside her robe.

A giggle threatened to ruin the moment. She tried to ignore it.

Logan lifted his head. "What?"

"Nothing." She cleared her throat. The giggle came out in a whoosh. "You taste like Cap'n Crunch."

"Is that right?" He gave the belt a good tug and her robe fell open. His gaze locked on her hardened nipples. "What have we here?"

His lips barely grazed her right breast when his phone rang. Up on the living room wall, the text showed the call was coming from McCabe Security and Investigation.

8

LOGAN FROWNED, AND it was such a rapid transition, it made Kensey step back. It was doubtful the caller could see all the way into the kitchen but she quickly retied her sash.

"I have to take this." Logan was already on his way to the living room, where he took a seat on the couch and accepted the call. "Mike," he said. "It's late. What are you doing at the office?"

"Okay, this is weird. I'm looking at you in your friend's apartment, right? Lisa told me to use your office phone if I needed to call you."

Logan sighed. "You know my sister. She wanted to see the place so she rigged the calls to go directly to Skype. It's pretty cool, though. I'm looking at you on a wall monitor in the living room. What's up?"

As Kensey cleared the table she glanced at the wall. Mike had short dark hair and a lean face shadowed with stubble. She put the milk in the fridge and carried the bowls to the sink, trying to ignore what was happening in the living room. Or that she and Logan were wearing matching bathrobes. If he'd wanted to speak privately he would've taken the call in his bedroom. Still, she didn't want to be nosy.

"I got a problem," Mike said. "You remember I told you about Tony? One of us. The Special Activities Division. Dude was burnt and left out to dry?"

"Yeah, sure. I remember."

"I saw him down at Rocco's Gym and he looked like shit. After he went too far in the ring, I pulled him aside. He's not doing well. He didn't tell me what had happened in Islamabad, but I could see why he'd been sent back. Bad PTSD. Permanent tremor, enough anxiety to fill a football field."

"I thought he was staying at that VA halfway house."

"He's been sleeping rough. Jumping at every noise. The dude needs some solid sleep and to get cleaned up. I don't think he remembers what it feels like to be human."

"Okay," Logan said. His voice was low, and he was rubbing his jaw as he seemed to think it over. Mike waited without fiddling around, his gaze squarely on Logan. The office around him was nothing special. Almost bleak but for a group of beautiful sunset pictures on the plain white walls.

"Take him to my place, if he'll go. Check out his meds. Then get Dr. Price to go talk to him. You know what to do, Mike."

"You think the doc will act on my say-so?"

"Why not?"

"You're always lead on these things."

"Hell, Dr. Price knows you. Probably knows all of us better than most people do," Logan said, with a quiet hollowness to his voice that filled Kensey with a sudden and inexplicable sadness.

"Okay. You know I'd take Tony to my place except all I've got is that efficiency."

"Don't worry about it. Like you said, he's one of us. Put him in the guest room and you take my room. Stay with him. But take care of yourself. Listen to your gut. You'll know if he's carrying. Explain the lockdown to him. He won't like it, but he's used to orders and regs."

Mike let out a humorless laugh. "No, he won't like it. But he knows me, so it shouldn't be too bad. I'll take care of him."

Kensey caught a glimpse of Logan's brief smile. And oddly, she thought she understood a little of what he was feeling. He had every right to be proud. Taking care of other vets was as much his mission as working to expand his business. And for that, she was proud of him, which was completely ridiculous. She'd met Logan only yesterday. But it wasn't as if she ran across men like him often.

"I know you will. Listen, buddy, you're more than ready for this. We get that contract and you'll be taking on more responsibility. Which you're also thoroughly prepared for."

"Wouldn't that be something?" Mike said. "Getting the contract, I mean. Have you seen Holstrom yet?"

Kensey froze. The glass she was holding nearly slipped out of her hand.

Holstrom? Had she heard correctly? What business could Logan have with—

Oh, God. The contract he so desperately wanted.

Was this some kind of sick cosmic joke? Of all the companies for Logan to be going after, why did it have to be Holstrom's? Although it made sense since Holstrom was the largest arms dealer and defense contractor in the country. And Logan had a very aggressive plan to expand quickly.

Silence hung over the room. No one was talking.

Lost in her own thoughts, she hadn't realized the call

had ended. She cautiously glanced over her shoulder. Logan stood at the window looking out, his voice a low murmur.

No, he hadn't disconnected the call but had switched to his cell phone. For privacy, she imagined. Was it because he didn't want her to hear about his dealings with Holstrom? That made her nervous. Even if Logan's sudden secrecy had nothing to do with her, personally, it could mean he knew Holstrom wasn't completely on the up-and-up.

She hoped not. She so wanted Logan to be one of the good guys.

With the last of the dishes loaded in the dishwasher, she tightened the belt on her robe, unsure what to do next. She took in the breadth of Logan's shoulders, the narrowness of his waist, and hips the thick robe couldn't hide. The backs of his calves were visible, tanned and solid with muscle. He probably ran ten miles every morning before getting around to his regular workout.

Logan wasn't just smart and ambitious, he was fit and disciplined and knew how to control his ego. Well, not when it came to showing her a thing or two about his agility, she thought, and allowed herself a small smile. But he didn't care about having his name in the paper or receiving credit for his work. Maybe his strength of character came from operating in the shadows for most of his adult life. It didn't matter. She was damn good at reading people and Logan hadn't been faking all that passion burning in his eyes when he'd spoken of his fellow vets. He was nothing like Holstrom.

Which begged the question…how much did Logan really know about the man he wanted to do business with? Had they already met? Did they have any kind of relationship? Or did Logan know only what the public was fed by Holstrom's very clever PR staff?

To the world, Holstrom was a huge success story. Totally legit businessman. If not for the whispered rumors filtering through her smaller circle, she would have never thought any differently.

She stared at Logan's back, unsure what to do next. She knew how he expected the rest of the evening to go. Sex had been at the top of her list, as well, until five minutes ago. Even now her body longed for the warmth of his touch. Just thinking about his skilled mouth made her lips part. But did she trust her brain to remain detached? Could she hide the uncertainty and fear building inside her?

He probably had no idea the man he was so desperate to work with was a thief…well, an alleged thief. Although the more she learned about Holstrom, the more convinced she was that it was true. But then proving Holstrom had possession of the Degas was the only hope she had of helping her father. Still, if she was right, which she honestly believed she was, hording works of art for his own pleasure spoke volumes about the kind of man Holstrom was, and for the life of her, she couldn't imagine Logan sending any of his people to work in Holstrom's world.

But perhaps that, too, was just wishful thinking. She had no way of knowing if Logan would simply rationalize Holstrom's behavior. After all, Logan had told her he was more interested in the bigger picture. Interested enough to overlook Holstrom's transgressions? That was impossible to know unless she came out and asked Logan. No way could that happen. She'd open herself up to all kinds of questions.

And she was in no position to provide answers. Not without setting herself up. It wasn't as if she was lily white in all this. If she was lucky enough to get a glimpse of the Degas in Holstrom's possession, she would do everything in her power to expose the man.

Even if it meant Logan's deal would blow up in his face. Dammit.

Why hadn't she kept her distance? Well, she sure as hell had no choice but to stay away from him now.

God, fate could be so damned cruel. She liked Logan. She'd even dared to consider what might happen once they returned to New York. They both led busy lives which involved travel, but that wasn't necessarily a bad thing. In fact, it could have turned out to be the perfect arrangement. No strings. No expectations. Great sex.

But now...

She moved toward her bedroom, lingering in the hall to take one last look while he was still engrossed in his conversation. She couldn't hear what he was saying, which was just as well.

Then she slipped into her bedroom, quietly closing the door behind her. He might knock, but she hoped the shut door was message enough.

Most likely Logan knew nothing about the man beyond his shrewd business dealings, and it was difficult for anyone to argue with his success. If Holstrom offered Logan the contract, would he still want it if he did know? Was he right to put his vets first, and take the money, regardless of the morals of the man giving it to him?

She was tempted to call Neil and get his take. But it was late, and he was busy. And she needed to really think about how much she wanted to reveal. Tomorrow would be soon enough. Tonight, she was going to give herself some quiet time to figure things out before she faced Logan again.

It pained her to admit it, but she had to consider the possibility that Logan's connection to Holstrom might be of use to her. If all else failed, that link could be her way in.

Great. What did that say about her own morals?

ONCE HE WAS off the phone with Mike, Logan found the kitchen empty. Kensey had obviously been busy. The table was cleared, the cereal and milk put away and the dishwasher loaded. He'd been so deep in conversation with Mike that he hadn't heard her.

She was probably in his room, waiting. God, he hoped so. Just thinking about her in his bed was making him hard. Forget about replaying what she could do with that lush mouth of hers.

No Kensey in his room or his bathroom. Which led him to standing outside her door.

Her closed door.

Maybe she was just changing. Or brushing her teeth, which he should have done. He almost went back to do just that, but then if she came out looking for him, she might think he wasn't interested in having part two of their evening, so he waited.

She was awfully quiet. And it didn't look as if a light was on.

Finally, it came down to leaving or knocking. He wasn't crazy about either option. But he wanted to talk to her. If he'd said something or done something…maybe she felt insulted that he'd been on the phone for so long. But he doubted that. Kensey wasn't the type to get huffy over him taking a work call.

Maybe he should knock. Just once. If she didn't answer, or if no light came on, he'd go back to his own room and that would be that.

Disappointed and confused, he stood there for another minute before he turned and walked down the hall. At first he'd thought it was cool that Sam programmed the floor tiles to illuminate with each footfall. But the lighted path he retraced to his room cast weird shadows on the walls.

The plain white walls.

He'd never seen them turn an eerie shade of white before. What the hell did that mean?

9

STILL DRINKING THE coffee he'd bought a block away, Logan entered the exhibition hall. The place was already crowded, but then it was already on the late side.

This morning he'd discovered another excellent feature the apartment offered. Sensors had picked up that he'd awoken and the coffee he'd forgotten to program the previous night had been ready by the time he shuffled to the kitchen. He'd hoped the scent would have lured Kensey out of her room. Hell, for all he knew, she'd left before he'd gotten up. The door to her room had remained closed.

He'd taken the taxi he'd planned on sharing with her, his mood sullen, the temptation high to give in to his hurt feelings.

But what possible good could it do? He'd come to this conference feeling excited. There was so much riding on the outcome of the next couple of days: his presentation, his meeting with Holstrom. The tightness in his gut was familiar, built over years of combat conditions. It was his engine, that tightness. It made him quicker, smarter, more careful.

So what the hell was he doing, mooning over someone he barely knew? Yes, the sex last night had been incredible—

possibly the best he'd ever had—and if it turned out to be just a one-night stand, he'd visit that memory often. Not his disappointment.

Besides, his mind needed to be on work. Taking down names, getting business cards. There was such a wealth of opportunity in this loud, overcrowded convention hall.

He also needed to check out the room where he'd be speaking tomorrow to get a feel for it. It just so happened someone he respected was giving a presentation on "Future Crimes in a Connected World" at 4:00 p.m. in the same room, so he figured he'd wait until then.

But most of his day would be spent checking out booths and collecting brochures. He'd stopped by Holstrom's booth yesterday, to take a quick look at what he was showcasing. There had been a lot of impressive stuff. And since Logan hadn't slept much last night, he'd done some poking around online. Today he had a few questions for the reps.

He knew that his future didn't depend on the Holstrom contract, even if it felt like it did. Logan had faced so much during his career. This was just another challenge. And so, evidently, was Kensey. God*damn it*, he had to find out her last name.

For the umpteenth time he wondered what had made her disappear without a word. Maybe she'd gone to check her messages and had a work problem to deal with. Or she'd fallen asleep.

Nah, he hadn't been on the phone that long.

It still bothered him, that comment about black ops. It wasn't the first time he'd been asked about that by civilians. He'd never given it much thought. But with Kensey...

Something was going on with her, and his gut told him the black ops remark wasn't simply a misunderstanding.

She'd set off his radar in more ways than one. But there was nothing he could do about it. Not here, not now.

The last two sips of his coffee had gone cold. He needed more caffeine, pronto.

Turning right, he made mental notes as to which booths he'd come back to visit. When he heard his name being called from a booth up ahead, he grinned. Only one person he knew could yell like a quarterback and look like a shy, sweet thing.

His pace quickened and there she was, up ahead, right before a log jam of conference goers. Sam O'Connel, with her unmistakable long wavy hair the color of a copper penny. She'd named her business SOC Electronics, a riff on her name. But SOC was also an acronym for Special Operations Command in the military, as well as a computing term. A device called a System-on-Chip integrated all the components of a computer into a single chip.

They'd all called her Soc in college. They were right to. He'd never known anyone to have tackled so many areas of computing or electronics and been so successful.

Hell, designing the smart apartment was what she did for fun.

She stood outside her large, crowded booth, her smile as big as ever, but man, she'd changed. Her image on the apartment's wall monitor hadn't done her justice.

The closer he got, the better she looked. Who would've guessed she'd blossom in her thirties? No, Sam was younger than him and the rest of the gang. Twenty-nine, maybe? The whiz kid had been a college freshman at fourteen.

"Logan. You look good."

"Me?" He wrapped her in a big hug. "You went and got gorgeous. When did that happen?"

"I don't know," she said. "Probably when you started needing glasses."

He held her at arm's length. "Sorry. Twenty-twenty vision all the way. You are seriously beautiful."

She blushed, turning so pink her cheeks almost matched her hair.

"Makeup and a sexy dress? Is this the new you? Or are you just trying to impress me?"

"Yeah, right." Sam grinned. "I'm glad to see you're still in one piece. How about my furniture? You didn't break anything last night, did you?"

"Smart ass." Logan had forgotten about his SOS call. "Yeah, we don't need to ever bring that up again."

"Fine. But no more cracks about the dress and makeup," she said as she led him to the booth's entrance. "I was interviewed earlier for *Security Management* mag. Why they didn't want to photograph me in my work uniform, I'll never know."

"Your work uniform consists of tights and nerdy T-shirts. Unless things have truly changed in your world."

"Nope. You ought to try it out. With your legs? You'd look hot."

Once he was inside her booth, he understood why there were so many people waiting to talk with her. She was Steve Jobs mixed with Nikola Tesla. SOC Electronics dealt in everything from biometrics to nonlethal weapons. Sam also worked on the cutting edge of prosthetic animatronics, and she'd made him a burglar-proof lock for his ten-speed back in school that he used to this day.

Luckily for Logan, the four people manning the booth were doing all the meeting and greeting. He didn't know the three women but he recognized the guy from their MIT days...

"You remember Clark Draper?" Sam said.

"Sure do." Logan shook his hand. Now *he* looked like a computer geek. It was clear he didn't wear ties very often, or get any sun. He'd signed on with Sam during junior year. He'd taken her messages, made her appointments and herded her to class, while she collected multiple degrees and invented things.

"It's good to see you, Clark," he said. "You still have that model plane collection?"

"Yep."

"Excellent."

From what Logan remembered of Clark, he wasn't much of a conversationalist. At least in this kind of setting. Get him alone and he could be pretty interesting. Logan turned his attention back to Sam.

She led him behind a big table display of computers, all of them showing off her latest gadgets in 3D. Set in the back away from the crowd were two director's chairs, and they sat close to each other so they wouldn't have to yell over the din.

"So, how are things at the apartment?"

"Un-effing-believable. It's like moving in with the Jetsons, only much better. Sam, I'm not kidding. People would pay up the wazoo to have that bathroom alone. And the kitchen? I've proposed to the coffee maker. Still waiting for an answer."

Sam laughed. "Did you see the mac and cheese and the Cap'n Crunch?"

"What do you think I had for dinner last night?"

"Oh, God, really? And Kensey?"

"Frosted Flakes."

"Huh. Now, that surprises me."

Logan was tempted. It was the perfect opening. Sam obviously knew a little more than she'd let on about Kensey.

"So, about the walls changing colors," Sam said. "You think it's too much?"

"Jesus, girl. You knocked it out of the park. I mean, come on. That's going to be standard for every house in the world before you can blink. You're going to make a fortune."

She grinned, flushed and happy, then looked at her feet. "I'm still not sure I'm going to make it public. I don't like the idea of strangers staying there."

"Well, if it bothers you, I'll try and come to Boston as frequently as possible so I can stay there. Although, you really will miss out on a fortune."

She shrugged, then met his gaze again. "I've got money. My own now."

Logan wasn't sure what she meant. He thought her parents had kept her in popcorn and Diet Mountain Dew until she'd set up shop.

"I never told you about my seed money, did I?"

He shook his head.

"Neil Patterson."

"Okay." Logan knew the name, and wondered if Patterson was the man Kensey had worked for, as well, if that was the connection between them.

"He saw my thesis project."

"The face recognition program?"

"Yeah. He said he thought I showed some talent and we worked it out. Neil was my only revenue source for a few years. He was very patient and even helped me learn the business side of things. Helped Clark, too. Now we're all making a bundle."

"That's great. Really great." A piece of the puzzle almost fit but something was off. Kensey had tensed when she'd mentioned her former employer, so Logan had assumed their split had been less than amicable. "Did Kensey used to work for him? Is that why she's staying at the apartment?"

Sam's eyes closed. "Please don't ask me about any of that. He's never asked me for anything. It's been straight up business this whole time, nothing personal. So when he asked for this, I said yes. He could have asked me to let her live there for the rest of her life, and I'd have said yes. She's nice, though. I mean, she's been nice on the phone. Did she do something horrible? Please say no."

"No. Not horrible. Just odd."

"The black ops thing? Because I don't think she meant anything by it, Logan. Honestly. I would tell you if she did."

He shook his head.

Sam put her hand up. "I knew it. It's got to do with that horny business. I hope someone else can help you with that, 'cause it's not going to be me."

Logan couldn't help laughing.

"Shut up." Blushing, she smacked his arm. "I didn't mean it like that."

"Like what?" Logan braced himself for the next assault. The rest of the old college gang would be so proud. Their little sister was growing up. Five years ago the conversation would've gone over Sam's head. "Okay," he said when she glared at him. He'd bet she could program the apartment for some mean payback. "Sorry."

Ah, she wasn't glaring anymore. Sam had returned to geek mode.

"You know, I think it might be possible to synthesize an aerosol that can make people horny," she said absently, and then blinked. "Look, Logan, one thing I know for sure. I trust Neil down to my bones."

"Fair enough." He found it a little disconcerting that Sam put Neil Patterson first, but it made sense. Logan and Sam were old friends, but they led such disparate lives. The great part was, whenever they did see each other they were always able to pick up right where they'd left off.

"So tell me what else is new? Didn't you mention something really big?"

"Oh, it's major, all right," she said. And then she almost smiled.

"This is gonna be good. I know that look."

She held up her arm. He'd wondered about the bracelets. She wasn't a jewelry kind of person. But clearly she'd
changed. There were four silver bangles just above her
wrists. They were very slim and had interesting markings.

He leaned in for a better look. "Are those hieroglyphs?"

"No, but you're not far off." She moved her chair closer.
"One of these, when slipped from your wrist, turns automatically into a three-hundred-and-sixty-degree camera.
And all the data is sent directly to a master hub, where
it's encrypted with some wicked new software I'll tell
you about later."

She stopped, caught her breath and then she was going
again. "But it doesn't have a limit on how much data it
can gather, because it just flows through to Mama Bear.
And there can be a chain of data collectors, an infinite
number, because of the cloud system I'm using. It's so
detailed that the operator, Mama Bear, would be able
to re-create every inch of space in a given room. It self-
generates forward motion, which is done by nano chips
that I can't tell you about because that money's already
spoken for. Anyway, that doesn't matter. Just, it'll never
run out of steam. Think a Roomba that picks up pictures
instead of dirt and hairs."

"Holy shit."

She nodded. "The hieroglyphs tell her what direction
to go in. What kind of landscape she'll have to maneuver. She can only move if there are no people present. No
strangers, actually. If she's working for you, you'll have a
marker that lets her know you're cool with her doing her
thing. Although you'd better not do anything gross, like
some people I could mention." She glared at Clark, who
ignored her completely.

Jesus. It slowly registered for Logan. His mind was

scrambling in several directions. Yeah, he'd call this break-through pretty major.

"I'm working on audio, but that still needs some tweak-ing, so we're not sharing that yet. In fact, you, Neil, Clark and I are the only people in the whole world who know about her so far. She'll be getting her big debut on the last day of the conference."

Before Sam had finished talking, Logan had thought of ten viable uses for this device. The possibilities were endless. It could save a lot of lives.

"Hey," Clark said, from behind Logan.

Sam checked her watch and stood up. "I'm sorry, Sol-dier Boy. I have to go. I have another interview," she said. "But I'll see you later, and we'll catch up on you, okay?"

He stood and gave her a brief hug. "Later."

She ran off, and Logan spent some time looking at her newest crop of goodies, mingling with the swirling crowd built entirely of Sam fans. Goddamn, he wished she'd go public. Although she didn't need to. Good for her. She worked as hard as anyone he'd ever—

Kensey.

He spotted her down the aisle, carrying a briefcase. Her hair was pulled back, and she looked like those models who showed up in magazine ads, pretending to be typi-cal working women. Her dress was green, sleeveless and showed off a lot of leg. Every guy in sight stopped what they were doing and watched her. She just kept walking, her confidence both a dare and a warning.

By the time he could see her dress was suede, he'd for-given her everything.

Then she stumbled a tiny bit.

Because she'd seen him.

Damn it to hell, she turned around and started walk-ing away, and that really pissed him off.

Bullshit.

He made his way through the bustle, completely un-
willing on every level to let her get away with this. No
way, no how, were they gonna dance her dance.

"Kensey," he called, and her stride slowed.

She was debating letting him chase her down. What
the hell? He'd been dismissed more kindly by Afghan
militants.

Then she stopped.

It didn't help his mood, knowing she hadn't wanted to.

WHY? KENSEY CLENCHED her jaw so hard she might have
broken a tooth. Why had she come down this aisle when
she knew it was possible Logan might be hanging out
at Sam's booth? Why couldn't she have seen him first?

She hated this. Hated that what she really wanted to
do was take him straight home to bed, and not leave until
this whole week was over. Sure, she wouldn't be helping
her father, but he'd never done much to help her, either.

Just thinking that made her stomach twist into a knot.

This wasn't a problem her father had created. She'd
heard the name Holstrom last night, and that was it—she'd
freaked. She had no way of knowing what Logan's connection with the man was or what he knew about him. It
could very well be nothing. It was too big a risk to take.
To like him so very much.

But who was she so attracted to? The sweet, funny,
amazing lover? Or the dangerous man who'd been the
kind of soldier who wasn't allowed to talk about the things
he'd done.

"Hello, Kensey," he said.

She gave him a brief smile. "I was just coming to see
Sam, actually. I wasn't expecting to see you."

"I could tell."

Kensey gave him nothing. No reaction. Inside, though,

a maelstrom was raging. Logan had no business looking so good. Feeling so betrayed. She should apologize. Make up an excuse. Ask him what he was doing with Holstrom.

Sam vouched for the man in front of her. Neil vouched for Sam. Which didn't mean Logan wasn't in Holstrom's pocket. It didn't seem likely, but then Logan was a chameleon. She understood that. So was she.

Her father's daughter.

It would be her own fault if she let this man get under her skin. There was no one else she could blame. "Well, actually, I have to go. There's a presentation…"

"Right." He made a point of looking at his watch. She knew it was two-thirty and all the presentations started on the hour. "Well," he said, shrugging. "See you around."

"Wait." The word was out before she could stop it. She didn't know what to say but she couldn't leave it like this.

He slowly turned back to her. "Don't worry. I get the message. For what it's worth, it's a shitty way to tell me to get lost."

"Last night, I was just trying to give you some privacy. And then I heard something about work and…"

Logan stared at her as if he couldn't believe how lame the excuse was, and she didn't blame him. But spending any more time with him wasn't a good idea. "I have something tonight and I have no idea what time I'll be home. Back," she corrected. "But if you're free and still up, we could have a nightcap."

He nodded, but from his expression it was clear he wasn't expecting much, which was for the best. She'd only wanted to extend an olive branch. Leave things between them on a more cordial note. Tonight she'd wait him out. Return after he was asleep. He'd understand she got caught up in whatever.

When he walked away without saying goodbye, it stung.

AT MIDNIGHT, LOGAN finished the single bottle of Pliny he'd allowed himself to have while he reviewed his presentation notes. He'd been back at the apartment for almost an hour after having dinner with a couple of old friends. He hadn't mentioned his plans to Kensey. Why bother? She had no intention of having that nightcap. Hell, he'd known she'd only made the offer to smooth things over. What he couldn't decide was whether or not to force the issue. Stay up. Call her bluff. Find out what the hell had happened last night.

He gathered his notes, turned off his tablet and switched off the lamp. The soft glow of the lighted tiles would be enough to get him to his room. Of all the apartment's cool surprises, the tiles were way up on the list. Walls turning into monitors to receive calls might be his favorite, though. He was still on the fence about the body sensors.

Halfway to his room he heard the front door open. It barely made a sound but he had exceptional hearing. Suddenly, he didn't like the illuminated tile so much. She saw him right away. And she didn't look happy about it.

"Hi." She closed the door behind her. "I'd hoped to be back earlier." She moved a few steps into the foyer. "I didn't want to wake you."

"I was just headed to bed."

"Please, don't let me keep you."

"I didn't intend to." Logan wasn't surprised she was anxious to be rid of him, and her body language was still shutting him down cold.

"Look, I'm sorry. It wasn't intentional."

He nodded. At least he was sure she wasn't a plant here to keep tabs on him. "Maybe tomorrow?" she said.

"Maybe." He wouldn't hold his breath.

10

THE LARGE BALLROOM was packed. Even if Kensey had wanted to sit down, it didn't look as if there were any seats left. She'd wanted to stay near the exit, but so many others had come after her that she'd been shuffled almost all the way to the end.

Logan looked good in the front of the room. He wasn't using the podium. In fact, he was walking as he spoke, making continuous eye contact with people in both the front and the back. He must have given a prepared speech before she'd come into the room, but this was better. He'd asked for questions just as she arrived, and thirty minutes later, he was still fielding them.

Wow, he was terrific. Passionate. Engaging fully with the audience.

The only problem was her wandering attention. Despite his riveting presence, she'd zoned out, remembering the body underneath his fashionable suit. Remembering all too vividly how it had felt when he was inside her.

"I absolutely agree. Not every veteran will be a good fit for security work. But if you believe they could fill another need within your organization, why not give them the chance? The thing you know for sure is they've learned to follow orders," Logan said and got some laughs and nods.

"And if you've got any concerns about their mental readiness, it's okay to tell them they should go to counseling now, and to come back later. That'll be completely up to them. But have the names and numbers of qualified therapists available. If you need help with that, call my office. It's important to remember the skill set that leads to a successful military career. Especially during times of war. Don't cut them—or yourself—short."

Logan pointed to a man in the fifth row. "Question?"

A tall man in a gray business suit rose. "Can you give us some signs to look for? I mean for PTSD?"

"I've put some brochures on the back tables that discuss the symptoms. You might consider adding a psychological profile in your application process. I can help you with that. Help any of you with that."

More hands shot up. A quick look at her watch told Kensey he was running over timewise. Next year, he would need a bigger room and a second hour.

"I see I'm out of time," he said. "I know a lot of you are veterans who've had difficulty finding meaningful work. And I know there are CEOs and HR executives who are here because you'd like to support the troops in the best way possible. Please register for our database, and if you have questions, I'm happy to address them. I know what good men and women can do after they've served. We are a force to be reckoned with. Thank you."

Kensey joined in the enthusiastic applause, kicking herself for missing the beginning of his session. But she'd gotten a call from Neil. He'd told her Seymour had sold another painting—a Van Dyck. Nothing near as pricy as the Degas, but it would pay the bills for another few months. She'd hoped for much more. All Neil could say was that things were in motion. Yeah, that would be her head spinning.

She gave up the idea of a quick getaway when her row hadn't moved for five minutes, but she wasn't that worried about being seen because Logan was surrounded by people hoping to speak with him.

It was easy to understand why Holstrom was interested in Logan. And after hearing him speak, it seemed even more impossible to her that Logan knew who Holstrom really was. If Logan got the contract, and she exposed Holstrom, what then? Would Logan be painted with the same shame-filled brush?

Having moved about a foot, she finally got a look at what the holdup was. Something had gone wrong with a wheelchair. A few men behind her had climbed over the row of seats in front and were heading to the other exit. In the dress she was wearing, she didn't dare.

Her gaze went to Logan again. He was smiling, shaking hands. Talking.

She closed her eyes for a moment and centered herself. Just because Logan fit her idea of what a good man was, didn't make it so. She didn't know him. Coming to this presentation had been idiotic. But she'd had to do something to take her mind off her plan to prove Holstrom to be the true owner of the original stolen Degas. Which would all be for nothing if Holstrom didn't call her. It was already day three. There had to be another way to get on his radar.

Finally, the line moved. When she was almost at the exit, Logan's voice came clear up to the back row. "Kensey."

It felt horrible, but she needed to keep walking. There were still people around him.

When her phone rang, she winced. Probably Logan, asking her to wait, but no, it was Sam. Asking her if she was free to come to her booth. Thank God.

She replied to Sam with a big yes, then without looking in his direction, texted Logan and told him she was on her way to Sam's booth.

Once she was free of the room, guilt settled in her cells. She made her way through the crowd mobbing the booths, a jungle of noise and riotous color.

There was Sam's booth. Kensey hadn't realized how large it was yesterday. God, today was only Wednesday. Minutes felt like hours while everything was happening way too fast.

There were several people manning the booth, but it was easy to spot Sam with that glorious head of hair. She'd put it up in a twist, but a number of coppery tendrils had broken free. It had the effect of giving her a sort of halo. She looked great.

There were three men talking to her, all in suits that looked more tailored than what Kensey expected to see on the exhibition floor.

Sam, though…

No wonder they looked spellbound. Kensey had no idea what she was telling them, but she was putting her heart and soul into it. Her arms were waving all around, as if she was conducting an orchestra. From the little Kensey knew about Sam, she didn't get out much. Almost never. What a shame—she was a joy. Thankfully, the men left before long. Sam turned to see Kensey waiting, and her eyes widened with welcome.

"Come on in," Sam said, leading her to the booth's entrance. Once they were inside, Sam stuck her hand out. "It's so great to meet you in person. Do you want something to drink? Someone's going on a coffee run in a minute. I was delusional when I thought one thermos of caffeine was going to be enough."

"I'd kill for a giant latte with two extra shots."

"Done." Sam pointed to a chair in the back of the booth,

but she didn't join Kensey until she'd texted the addition to their order. Then she plopped onto the director's chair. "I swear this week is going to kill me."

"I can't imagine. There are always so many people at your booth."

"That's the problem. I have to think of a way that I won't have to be here next year. When it's finally over, it takes me a long time to adjust to my regular routine. I loved that I got to see Logan, and now I get to meet you, though. Neil thinks the world of you."

Warmth filled Kensey's chest. "The feeling's mutual, I assure you. He's been wonderful to me. Both of you have. The apartment, my God, I've never seen anything like it. I know squat about computer stuff. I can get what I need to out of a MacBook Air, and when something goes wrong, I know who to call."

"I'm the exact opposite. It's the insides that make me happy. I fell in love with computers when I was just a kid. Gaming mostly, then figuring out how they worked. Then, in college, I started inventing things. If you don't mind, I'd love to know what you like most about the apartment, and if there's anything you find too intrusive or whatever."

"The combination of colors and scents and music was a little spooky, at first, but amazing once I realized what was happening. At first I really thought someone, well, you, were watching me."

Sam let out a laugh, and then covered her mouth. "Sorry. The cameras activate only when the place is empty. I can see how the mood sensors might be confusing. I need to work on a brochure or something that explains what's triggering the colors and sounds. Although it's kind of fun surprising people, too."

"And giving them heart attacks?"

"No," Sam said, grinning, "that would be bad for business. Did Logan tell you about calling me to turn off whatever was making him horny?"

Kensey felt her jaw slacken. "Umm…no."

"Oh." Sam turned pink.

Kensey was pretty sure her face was a perfect match.

"Don't mind me," Sam said. "Really. Sometimes I say the craziest things. The guys used to tease me about having no internal filter. What do you think about the music?"

It took Kensey a second to pick up the thread. "Oh, it's so interesting. I have favorite songs I use for my yoga so I overrode the music the first day, but the second time, I wondered what would happen if I let the apartment decide. It was great! Better than the music I'd compiled. I felt completely relaxed and focused. Some lights dimmed, and then the windows darkened! The apartment seemed to learn so much about me after hearing my music once. Is that possible?"

"That's what it's supposed to do."

"Artificial intelligence, right?"

Sam winced in a way that told Kensey she was close but no cigar. "Yeah. Kind of."

"Wow. Also, the shower? The bathtub? Everything in that gigantic bathroom? I'm going to cry when I have to leave. It's perfect."

"That makes me really happy. Thank you. I keep fiddling with it. I'm using all the guys as guinea pigs, which is great because it means I get to see them without having to get on an airplane."

This was the second time Sam had referred to "the guys" and now Kensey was curious. "I assume you mean Logan and other college friends?"

Sam nodded. "I was only fourteen when I started at MIT. I didn't know anybody. And no one wanted to hang out with a kid. But that was okay. I wasn't very social, anyway. Well, until I met Logan."

"How long have you two been friends?"

"Since freshman year, so that would be almost fifteen years."

"Wow. Long time."

"We were a gang. Logan, Rick, Matt and me. None of us were studying the same thing, but we all lived in the same dorm at MIT. There was a big screen TV in the lounge and we kept showing up for the same shows—stuff like Adult Swim, *Family Guy*, *The Tick*, *Buffy*. We all laughed at the same jokes. Then we started hanging out. After Logan went off with the army, Matt and Rick decided to rent a house together, and they included me.

"When I met them, it was the first time I really had friends. I didn't realize until later how much they looked out for me. Logan would get mad when I would forget to eat or lost track of time on the computer and stayed up too late." Sam grinned. "I used to call him Mom."

Kensey smiled. It wasn't easy talking about Logan. "Are you still close to the other two, as well?"

"Yes. Rick for sure." Sam frowned. "Is something wrong?"

"No." Kensey straightened, aware she might have sounded wistful, which wouldn't do at all. "Nothing. I was just thinking about how much we have in common. I didn't have friends either when I was growing up—I still don't, really." She shouldn't have added that last bit. It was her own fault she wouldn't let anyone close.

"You? No way."

"Well, that isn't true. I have Neil. He's great. I don't know what I'd do without him. He's not just my boss. He's a good friend."

"For me, too," Sam said. "I adore Neil. But I can't believe you didn't have friends in school. Or now."

"I was serious about my studies."

"Oh, I see." Sam rolled her eyes in a good-natured

way. "If not for the guys prying me away from my computer, my only social life would've been watching TV four times a week. And the weird thing is we aren't alike at all. Logan was so into the whole ROTC thing. He really believed in all that stuff—serving his country and making a difference. Not that I didn't, but back then I was too selfish. I'm still too selfish, probably. Then he was recruited away. But he should really be the one telling you this."

Kensey doubted he'd be telling her anything about himself at this point. "Has he changed much?"

"Not really. He had a tough time leaving the service. Went through a year that could have ended badly. Instead he found something else to believe in. Helping other vets come home and adjust. So, same Logan, different uniform."

Something tugged at Kensey's heart. Logan had gone through a bad year? She wanted to ask for details. She wanted to know everything…

No, she didn't. What she needed more than anything was to stay focused on what she was here to do. "What about you? Have you changed much?"

"Ha." Sam grinned. "I thought you were going to ask me about my love life."

"Oh, I was."

Sam choked out a laugh and looked relieved that their coffee order had just arrived. They each sipped their ventis in silence for a minute.

"I should go and let you get back to work," Kensey said. "But don't think I've forgotten about our conversation."

"What?" Sam blinked. "Oh. I'm still a card-carrying introvert who'd rather be in her lab than going on dates. But I love what I do. Guess you could say my work is my one true love."

"Oh, come on. That's just sad."

"And you should talk?" Sam said, laughing when Kensey muttered, "Touché."

"You have to come back and we can hang out some-time," Sam said. "You can stay in the apartment. I'll even take a couple days off."

"I have a feeling that's saying a lot."

Sam nodded as she stood up. "Don't tell anyone. Now I have to go talk to the chief information security officer for HBO. Call if you need me." She looked over Kensey's head. "Hi, Logan. Perfect timing, because I have to go."

Kensey stood, too, taken completely by surprise. Al-though she should've guessed he might show up. She had told him where she was headed.

Sam hugged him hard. "Be nice, okay? Be the sweetie I know you are." Then she let him go and spoke to them both. "Talk to you guys later."

THE SILENCE WASN'T really a silence because there wasn't any such thing in this crowded hall. But Kensey hadn't moved, or even sipped her drink after she'd seen him. She just stared.

"I confess I was glad I didn't know you were coming to my presentation. I would have been twice as nervous."

"You were amazing," she said, putting her coffee down on the chair without looking away. "I didn't even hear it all, but you made a big impression. I could tell. It was quiet. No one coughed. No texting. You had them riveted, and I imagine you'll get some good connections now, if not good offers."

Whoa. The last thing he'd have guessed Kensey would say was basically what she'd just said. The way it had all rushed out of her, as if he'd lifted a gate. If it was bullshit, or even practiced, he couldn't tell, and his life had de-pended on detecting things like that. Then again, this was Kensey, and his track record with her was lousy.

"Thank you," he said. "I imagine it works because I believe in what we're doing."

"Yes, you're right. But you also have a gift."

He shrugged, trying his damnedest to quash a grin. "I'm sorry we didn't have a chance to talk last night."

"Me, too," she said, and something had changed. Awareness flickered in her eyes.

"Do you have plans for this evening?"

She opened her mouth, but shut it again. Picked up her coffee, but didn't drink any of it.

"I have something I might have to do," she said. "But there's a chance it'll fall through. I should be home by six. If you're there…"

"I should be. I won't have to leave until around nine tonight, if I go. So, okay. We'll meet…maybe."

"Maybe," she said. A definite improvement, seeing as how they were both still staying under the same roof.

11

At 5:20 P.M., Kensey returned to the apartment and the most incredible bathroom known to humankind. It had an open shower that curved in a gradual downward spiral and made her feel as if she was at a spa the moment she started walking down the beautiful tumbled stone steps. The walls were made of glass tile, and as she passed, they—like the walls in the rest of the apartment—started changing colors.

A little farther on, there was a towel station and an amenities bar with everything from razors to salt scrubs. Then, as the path continued to curve, the wall colors got darker, greener, and the sounds segued from new age calm to a rainstorm with a dash of jungle.

Finally, she reached the shower itself. It had every possible kind of jet. The one that most impressed her was at the top of the enclosure, a big metal rectangle with lots of holes for the water to come through. The temperature was perfect. It was all perfect. The room smelled verdant and clean and, God knows, she hated to waste water, but this experience was like nothing else and she was going to enjoy the heck out of it.

She closed her eyes and all her troubles vanished. At

her fingertips was yet another shelf loaded with soaps, body wash, shampoo, loofahs and sponges. It all reminded her of *Willy Wonka* for hedonistic grown-ups.

She took her time smelling everything before she decided on what to use. It was a toss-up, but in the end she went with the coconut-scented body wash.

Lathering up awakened her senses to even more pleasure. Thoughts of Holstrom tried to take over, but she fought them back, not wanting to spoil a single moment.

When thoughts of Logan knocked, she threw the doors open in welcome. After hearing his presentation and talking to Sam, Kensey was feeling more relaxed about Logan. Given his goals, it made sense he'd want to hook up with Holstrom. He had all the connections: military, political and the private sector. For Logan to succeed, he'd need as many of those connections as possible.

Of course, if her suspicions about Holstrom and the stolen paintings turned out to be true, Holstrom and his company would certainly take a beating. Jail wasn't out of the question, although she doubted his corporation would fold. Logan could still come out of this a winner.

In the meantime, she had to find a way to get in front of Holstrom again. Soon. Maybe even tonight.

Her thoughts went back to Logan. Once he knew who Holstrom really was, he wouldn't want to work with him. He just wouldn't.

But she couldn't warn him off with no proof.

She started to shampoo her hair and she couldn't restrain her moan. Was it possible to stay in this shower forever? She'd end up a prune, but what did that matter when everything felt and smelt so fabulous. And who knew, maybe genius would strike. Some people sang in the shower, but Kensey had always used the time to problem solve. Talking out loud to herself helped her creativity and logic.

In this shower? Hell, she might come up with the cure for the common cold.

She let a few choice images dance behind her closed eyes as she massaged her scalp. Of course it was Logan she imagined. Naked. Hard and gorgeous. "Oh, hell, Logan. Why did you have to be here? Now. The timing's so bad." Sighing, she twirled in front of the twelve acupressure massage jets.

She rinsed. And for once she decided she would repeat before she started on the conditioner.

"Hot, hot, super-hot Logan," she said, loving the acoustics. If she'd had any kind of a voice, she'd have been singing instead of talking. "I mean where did that man go to lady parts school? He should be a full-on professor by now."

She rinsed off the second shampoo, humming a little "Voulez-Vous" before she added the conditioner.

"I mean," she went on, singing the first two words, then going back to her speaking voice because even she couldn't stand her off-key pitch. "Dammit, this is nuts. I'm going crazy trying to stay focused on what I'm supposed to be doing, and all I seem to think about is sex. With that amazing, intuitive, fearless man. And why, why hadn't I thought to wait until he came home so I could invite him in this shower with me?

"And…" The spray hit her square in the face and she jerked back, blinking. "This isn't solving anything."

"Uh, Kensey?"

She screamed. So loud and so long it hurt her own ears. Then she saw the wall. The goddamn wall had two monitors on it. One was her naked…oh, Christ…so naked. More naked than she'd ever been before, even with her hands over her tits. The other was filled by Logan. "What the hell?"

Logan cleared his throat. "I'm guessing you said, Call Logan?"

"I did no such thing."

He looked as if he was standing two feet away from her in his shirt, tie and slacks. Oddly, his feet were bare, but who cared about that when he was watching her with the same hunger from the other night.

"You must have, because once I accepted the call, there you were. I did try to get your attention."

"How, by sending a letter? I'm in the goddamned shower," she said, getting ready to unleash all the rest of her curse words in short order.

"I saw. But you were also talking to me."

"I wasn't. I was talking about you. Why didn't you say something?"

He chuckled low, sounding far too sexy. "Because it was hot? And you're gorgeous?"

"I am never speaking to you again. 'It was hot' is not a good excuse."

He shook his head, and she rolled her eyes. "There's nothing stopping you from turning around now."

He smiled. His hand went to his tie, and that was off in two seconds, followed by the quickest unbuttoning in the world. "I was invited," he said. He tossed his shirt behind him. Put his hands on his belt. "But if you want me to leave, I will."

"Does this thing do playbacks?"

He glanced at the monitors. "No idea."

"If it does, you have to destroy yours. Is that clear? No copies. And I don't want to hear a single solitary word you think was cute or funny or anything remotely like it."

He crossed his heart. On his very bare chest.

She lowered her hands. "Well, I suppose you can come in. But would you run and get a hammer out of the toolbox so I can pummel your memory to bits?"

"I don't know where the toolbox is."

"That's all right," she said, relaxing her shoulders. "I'll find it tonight when you're asleep."

"Fair enough."

She covered her face with her hands and shook her head. She loved that the tension had turned to something else, something almost playful, but she didn't understand why it required her to be humiliated.

"Hey, I'm taking off the important part here," he said.

"And…?"

"I'm only this way because of you."

"A gentleman would have said something."

"A gentleman would have been an idiot." He unzipped his pants, dropped those and his briefs in one step, and when he stood straight again, he really was impressively hard.

Then he closed his eyes in what looked like pure frustration and crouched down out of the frame. When he stood again, he held up three condoms.

"Optimistic?" she asked.

"Inspired," he replied.

She turned to the wall. "End Call you stupid, stupid computer." It blinked out before the sentence had ended. She thought she remembered now. She was pretty sure she had said, "Hell, Logan," but the water must've distorted her voice, making it sound like, "Call, Logan." Sometimes she really hated computers.

He joined her, all naked and fabulous. The apartment seemed to approve of its matchmaking as the tiles had gotten awfully colorful. And then, just audible over the sound of the jets, the background music started played "Sexual Healing."

She couldn't help but laugh. Until Logan pulled her into a kiss that could've melted the snow off all the mountains in the forty-eight contiguous states.

NOT ONLY WAS Kensey as beautiful wet as she was dry, she'd just given him the best explanation-slash-hard-on ever. But he was glad the monitors were off now and she was kissing him like there was no tomorrow. It had been a weird couple of days, but he was beginning to understand her disappearing acts. Too much sex on the brain had been a problem for him, as well. Right now all he wanted was to make them both feel good.

Running his hand down her neck to her chest, he lingered on the smooth skin underneath the warm water. Lingering over anything when he was this hard was difficult, but he wanted to make her desperate for it.

He cupped her breast and kneaded gently. This was exactly where he wanted to be. "You know you could have a career in film screams if you wanted one. That sounded like something from Hitchcock's collection. Very impressive."

"You would have screamed, too, if you'd been on my end of things." She winced. "It was loud, wasn't it?"

"I don't know. I'm thinking I could get you to top that." He smiled. "No terror involved."

She met his gaze and didn't move except to part her lips, which made him reach down and part her other lips.

"What are you—"

He kissed the question right off. Although he did like talking to her. When she wasn't being all mysterious, they were good sparring partners. Kensey was a lot of things he liked.

He liked how she looked all wet. He'd never understood why chick flicks made it appear as if kissing in the rain was sexy, but now he got it. Although it helped that this rain was hot, or maybe that was just Kensey.

The way her body pressed against him trapped his cock between them. Soon enough he realized there was a rhythm to the way she moved her hips, which matched each push of his fingers.

A quick look when he went to kiss her neck showed him that the damn walls were pulsing, too. Everything synchronized. It was compelling. Something he'd never experienced before.

He moved his lips to the shell of her ear. "Look at the tiles," he said.

A few seconds later, she said, "Oh, my God."

"I know." Then, as a little experiment, he pumped a little faster.

She matched his pace, thrust for thrust. It took a few seconds, but the walls joined in, along with a sudden deep blue coming from the showerhead above them. By that time, though, he wanted more than pretty lights and hot water.

As he slipped his fingers out of her wet heat, he bent over, the water sluicing down his back as he took her nipple in his mouth. He tasted water first, which somehow made things even sexier, until he tasted Kensey. That outdid everything. It was a precise taste, not just skin. *Kensey's* skin. His mouth filled with want for the rest of her, the salty sea taste of her sex, the spot behind her ear that made her tremble.

He moaned, and he heard it as if they were in the ocean…no, a river heated by the sun, ripening her flesh and his desire.

Fingers touched the back of his head. Her palm seconds after. He wondered if her eyes were open. Was she watching him lick and swirl his tongue, with even a small idea of how much he wanted to both keep doing this and slide his cock inside her?

Soon, that wasn't enough, either. He rose and kissed her, pulling her body against his, not just to show her how hard he was, but to let her know what he wanted.

She surprised him, though. Her hand slid between

them and curled around his cock. His head reared back. Luckily, he didn't choke on the spray from the shower-head, just coughed. He might have choked, though, the way she was rubbing him, slow and careful, putting a little more tension just under his glans, then swiping her thumb over the slit.

"You look pretty strong," she said, squeezing his bicep.

"I'm no body builder, but—"

"How about a body lifter? My body, I mean."

He smiled. "Not a problem." Although if she kept on with those strokes, he might not make it past putting on the condom. "Wait, I need a—"

She grinned. "You put them on the amenities tray."

"Don't go anywhere," he said, and reluctantly removed her hand while he went to grab the condoms.

Kensey had stayed right where she was, but she hadn't wasted the few seconds he'd been gone. She'd been touch-ing herself.

Damn. It was smoking hot.

He kissed her, hard, lifting her arms around his neck, then reaching under those gorgeous thighs and lifting her into position. Once he felt sure of his hold, he kissed her. Her lips were right there, so how could he skip that? A few minutes later, he said, "Reach between us? Guide me home?"

The look she gave him was meltingly hot, but her hand was already moving. This maneuver could be tricky, and just in case she lost her balance, he moved them close to the wall.

Although she was slim, she wasn't tiny, but she felt great in his arms. She moaned and laughed, then took his sheathed cock and guided him in the right direction. By the time she released him, he was good to go.

She tightened her legs around his hips, her arms around his neck.

"This will only be chilly for a moment," he said, surprised that his voice was so rough. He moved to the right, until the massaging jets hit him on the back, before he turned them around. Now, they were both getting the full experience of the overhead rain, and while he braced himself against the tiles, she would enjoy the massage.

He hoped that wouldn't be the best thing she felt.

"You're a genius," she said, raising herself up an inch or so, then relaxing her legs.

"And you're a gymnast," he said.

She laughed, and then started to ride him in earnest. He could feel her glutes tighten, which made her inner muscles squeeze him until he had to recite a few football stats so it wouldn't end yet.

But he didn't want her doing all the work. He was able to push in further, and she was free to concentrate on the right muscles.

"Good God, this is…" She finished the thought with a cry that made him forget his own name.

"We make beautiful music together, don't you think?"

"I can't carry a tune."

"You are so wrong," he said. "This is a symphony."

She let out a laugh, and they lost the rhythm, but only for a moment.

"You don't believe me? Listen."

She closed her eyes as he kept the pace languorous and sweet. He could tell the moment she heard a very real symphony coming from the hidden speakers all around them.

"Oh," she said. "Do you know this piece?"

"Not a clue. I just know we're conducting."

Her kiss was her agreement, and it spurred him to adjust her position. It wasn't easy, but she yelped when he hit the bull's-eye. Now when he lifted her and let her drop, he rubbed against her clit. The sounds she made were all he could hear. The panting *Ohs*, and then his name. Not just once. Escalating, as he went for broke. He didn't have long, but she fell apart first. Seconds before him.

And didn't that feel better than anything he could remember.

12

It took a long time for Kensey to catch her breath and find her feet as he let her down. Part of it was due to the raw sensations that still made her body thrum. It was amazing to her how in sync they'd been with each other. It had been effortless, which was at once thrilling and frightening.

When they'd been face-to-face, inches away from each other, something in her heart had shifted.

"You okay?"

Kensey turned her head to look at him. They were both leaning against the cold tile while the panel of jets blasted hot water across the wide shower to keep them warm in front. "Very okay. You?"

He grinned, then he leaned over to kiss her. "I'm waterlogged. How do you feel about moving this to the bedroom?"

She nodded, although this was a great stopping place. Truth was, she wanted to stay in bed with him. But she couldn't use Logan as a place to hide. She needed to figure out her next move with Holstrom, even though the thought made her queasy.

She turned off the shower while he went to gather towels. When they met up, he'd tied a small towel around his waist. The bath sheet in his hands was for her.

He wrapped the towel around her and started drying her body with it. It was tender and sexy all at once.

She grabbed a smaller towel for her hair, and he asked her to rate the showerheads from one to ten. It turned out to be a lot harder than she'd imagined, especially when he showed his disagreement by squeezing her butt or her boobs and making an obnoxious buzzer sound. She loved how they could go from being so passionate to flat-out silly in a matter of minutes. She surprised him, giving Logan Jr. a squeeze when Logan ranked the crisscross shower mists more highly than the massage jets. But they both gave the giant rain shower top marks.

With both of them reasonably dry and her bed calling to them, she took Logan's hand and led him into the adjacent room. The walls were soft again: pastel waves of blues, greens and purples. It was like being under the ocean, especially with the ceiling full of cotton-ball clouds dotting a perfect sky.

Dropping their towels, they scooted under the covers and made themselves a little nest in the center of the mattress. Logan's arms went around her, and her leg went over his thigh, touching as many places as possible.

Logan kissed her, ran his hand down her back, pressed close. He wasn't hard or anything, but that was fine. She liked this type of snuggling. Soft, sweet. The scent that had infused the room was intriguing.

"Petrichor," she said, happy she'd remembered the name.

"Am I supposed to make up a word now? *Quomalin.*"

"No. Petrichor is the scent of the earth after a rain shower."

"Really? That's an excellent word. And you're right.

That is what we're smelling." He turned his head toward the wall. "Good job, scent computer."

"Oh, you think it hears you? Dear God, I'll never make another sound."

"I think it's pretty safe."

She didn't have a ton of experience with men. She had too much to hide to let herself get too close to anyone. But if she could, she would like to have more of this. Of him. Maybe in New York?

It would be foolish to become invested in that idea, though.

"Where did you find your love of art?" he asked. "Boarding school?"

She shook her head. "My father," she said, and for the first time in years, she thought of him kindly. "He was so passionate about art that he wanted me to love it the way he did. With his whole heart. He used to take me to museums where he taught me to see that every painting has a story. How each person sees the work through their own experiences, so every story is different."

"That's…huh. The way you look when you talk about art makes me want to know more. I have zero experience with the arts. My family was amazingly boring."

"Are you close to them?"

"My parents? Nope. They live in South Carolina. We don't talk much. I gather you're close to your father?"

"I haven't seen him in a long time. And my mother died when I was young."

"I'm sorry."

"It's okay," she said. It was. Her mother wasn't a hot button.

"I haven't seen my folks for a while, either," he said, as he pushed back the stray hair she'd been seeing in her peripheral vision. "They're really into golf. It's all they do."

"How did you end up in the military?"

"It was a teacher, actually. In middle school. He loved everything about the service, although he was disabled and couldn't join up."

"Does he know that he inspired you?"

"No. He died when I was in boot camp."

"Sorry."

Logan shrugged. "He was great. I took to the army like a duck to water. I liked the discipline. The push to be a great soldier was very strong in me. I liked the challenge. So when I was recruited, I went for it."

"Why did they come for you?"

"I have a facility for languages. And trust me, I have no idea—"

Her phone rang. She couldn't afford not to get it. "Hold that thought?"

She went to her purse, which was on a chair alongside her briefcase. When she looked at the text, her heart started racing.

She felt nervous, of course, but also relieved. Holstrom had solved the problem of how she would meet him next. Unfortunately, it meant leaving the bed and Logan, which she was loath to do, but Holstrom was why she'd come to Boston.

"What is it?"

"I'm sorry. I was hoping… But I do have to go. I really do." She saw the disappointment in his face and thought once again how life could be so damn unfair. "You'll have to excuse me because I need to get dressed," she said and had to turn away.

HE NEEDED TO let this go already. Halfway to the hotel, and he was still gnawing on a dry bone.

Kensey had told him ahead of time that she might be called away, and it had happened. All he could think about was being shooed out of her room. One minute, he'd been completely relaxed and exactly where he wanted to be; the next, her door had closed behind him. He hadn't even collected the clothes he'd had on.

In practical terms, she'd done him a favor. His meeting with Holstrom was tomorrow. He needed to be in peak form. ASIS—the leading organization for security professionals—was having their reception at the Sheraton in about an hour, which would be a great way to learn more about the man.

Jim Barney, a veteran of the Gulf War, was in charge of recruiting high-level executives for Holstrom Industries Energy Division. Logan had met Barney in the HI booth, where he'd been talking about job openings and the many opportunities that existed within Holstrom Industries for the right people. He'd been very informative, entertaining and, yeah, they'd bonded over their military service. They'd made tentative plans to meet in the bar before going up to the reception.

Logan knew so much about Holstrom Industries that he could write a book, but his knowledge of the man himself was sketchier. It was common knowledge that he was a womanizer, and his reputation when things didn't go his way was part of his bigger-than-life aura. Barney had met Ian years ago, and he knew him pretty well.

After paying the taxi driver, he made his way to the lounge. Sure enough, Barney had found a stool at the bar and had a drink in hand. Walking the exhibit floor was paying off nicely, and Logan hoped this turned out to be an incredibly helpful chat.

Or Barney could tell his boss not to hire Logan.

"First one's on me," Barney said. "What's your poison?"

He wouldn't have minded a scotch, but he wasn't going to touch a drink until after his meeting tomorrow. "Tonic and lime."

"Really?" Barney's expression changed from vaguely interested to vaguely suspicious. "You in AA or something?"

"Or something."

"Well, hell." Barney sipped his drink. "I was gonna buy you another round, show you what a nice guy I am. But tonic and lime? Shit. I'll pick up your tab for the rest of the night."

"Thanks, but I'm fine. Just so I know we're on the same page, you still want to talk to me about Holstrom?"

"Yep. I got nothing there to hide, and you seem like a man who'd be an asset to the company. What do you want to know?"

"How you ended up where you are," Logan said. "What you think about the man."

Barney turned to face the room. "I'm gonna get us a table," he said. "That's a sitting down conversation." Logan ended up paying for his drink. An outrageous price for tonic water, but what the hell. Then he saw that Barney's poison was Johnnie Walker Blue. Fifty bucks a pop. But that didn't stop him from making sure the waitress would come by with another round in twenty minutes.

He didn't want to get Barney wasted. Just loose. The guy was in his fifties, and he looked more like a traveling vacuum salesman than a big-time recruiter for a major company. But with a gig like his, he had to be above reproach.

"About time," Barney said when Logan arrived at the table. "I was getting ready to invite a bunch of strangers to sit down."

Logan smiled. Put his drink down and shoved a small fortune in scotch whiskey across the table before he took a seat. "I didn't expect this kind of a crowd. I hope they aren't all going to the reception."

Barney nodded toward the back of the room. "Free buffet. Everyone crawls out of the woodwork for that."

"Aw, man. Thanks for reminding me I'm starving."

"That lime should fill the empty maw just fine until we get upstairs. Then you can eat to your heart's content."

Logan lifted his glass for a toast. "To veterans and assholes."

"Since I'm the senior vet…" Barney said, leaving the sentence right where it counted.

"Drink up."

The way Barney looked after taking a pretty serious sip of the scotch was just shy of embarrassing. He would have told the man to take his drink and get a room, but that was so cliché. "You've worked for Ian Holstrom for a long time. Why?"

Barney didn't blink at the question. "He pays me great money. You wouldn't think so, given the way I dress, but you added two and two together when you bought me this drink."

"That's it? Money?"

"No, son. That's not all of it. I find Ian Holstrom a unique individual. He wants the best people working for his company, and welcomes a challenge. Very few of the people I've helped to place quit. I don't know if they're happy, but they're making a good wage no matter what tier employee they are and their jobs are never boring. They're not working for HI because I felt sorry for them. They're extremely qualified and they're an intricate piece of the company. Finding someone who's the perfect fit can be taxing but also very satisfying. That's why I work where I work."

"That's a hell of a good reason," Logan said. "I have those goals myself. A good fit is important."

"And that's why we're having this conversation. I was there for most of your presentation."

That was a surprise. "You didn't say anything at the booth."

"Didn't need to. I also know you're in the running to be the new security subcontractor. You're smart to go after it and I think you have the best shot at it." Barney shrugged. "Don't get me wrong—I have no influence. He doesn't listen to me about security so I'm no help there. But he has connections that would make your company grow faster than any other way."

"That's what I'm counting on."

"Personally, I'd like to see you get the contract because of how many vets you'd be putting to work. I don't do that level of recruiting. My job is to go after a retired colonel or general, but you…you could be in a position to make a real difference. And here's how I can help you," Barney said, lowering his voice and leaning forward. "There's very little Holstrom likes more than to look good. If the public views him as patriotic or philanthropic, all the better. I'd play up the vet angle if I were you. How you can help him be the largest employer of ex-military in the country. Let him know how much people will eat that up. And the media, too. No need to be subtle about it, either. He won't care if you're using the angle to win him over. Hell, he'll respect you for it."

Logan nodded. He'd already planned to push the public-perception angle, but he liked knowing he didn't have to be sly about it.

The waitress came by with another drink for each man. When Barney reached for his wallet, Logan shook his head.

Barney nodded his thanks. "You know the story of the scorpion and the frog?"

"I… No. I don't think I do."

"Okay, so a scorpion and a frog meet on the bank of a wide stream, one the scorpion can't possibly cross. The scorpion asks the frog to carry him across on its back. The frog asks, 'How do I know you won't sting me?' The scorpion says, 'Because if I do, I will die too.'

"Satisfied with the scorpion's logic, the frog lets him jump on his back, and they set out, but halfway across the stream, the scorpion stings the frog. The frog knows he'll die without reaching the other bank, but he knows the scorpion will drown, too. The frog has just enough time to ask why.

"'Because,' the scorpion says, 'It's my nature.'"

Logan smiled. "I have been both the frog and the scorpion. But thanks for the reminder. At least I'll know what I'm getting into."

Barney nodded. "I think you'll do just fine."

LOGAN HAD EXPECTED the reception to be larger, and less fancy. "Small turnout."

"They don't invite everybody who has a booth," Barney said. "You have to have a certain size booth. You're here because of your presentation."

"Why are you here?" Logan looked at the man. His suit fit him well, and had to be more expensive than Logan originally thought. It was the guy underneath who was rumpled.

"As you know, I don't have a damn thing to do with security. I come here and talk to people. Ian hopes I'll steal talent from the competition. I'm heading to the buffet if you want to come with. They put out a really decent spread."

"Great. I really am starving—"

"By the way, don't corner Ian with business talk tonight. Save it for your meeting tomorrow. He doesn't like mixing business with pleasure, especially if he's got a knockout like her on his arm."

Logan followed Barney's gaze.

He spotted Ian Holstrom right away. He was standing near the bar looking sharp in a perfectly tailored dark suit. But that wasn't what gripped Logan's attention. Or sucked the air from his lungs.

It was Kensey.

She had her hand on Holstrom's arm. She was laughing at something, and the chandelier above them made her hair look like spun gold. Her dress wasn't like that last one, the one that had nearly given him a heart attack. This one was skintight. Red. Her stiletto heels were black and gave her a couple of inches on Holstrom.

She'd never said she knew the man.

But then why would she?

Logan struggled to remember if he'd said anything about Holstrom to her. No, he didn't think so. She knew he was after a contract, but he'd never said the name of the company. Had he?

Not likely. Hell, when he was with Kensey, business was the last thing on his mind. Different problem. So, no, she'd had no reason to mention she knew Holstrom. Unless she was involved with him, and then, yeah, it would've been nice if she'd said something before they'd had sex.

Shit.

She leaned closer to Holstrom.

Logan's blood pressure skyrocketed. What the hell was she doing?

"Hey, you interested in the buffet, or not?"

Logan looked at Barney and suddenly remembered something. Two nights ago. His phone conversation with Mike. Holstrom's name had come up. Directly after that, Kensey had gone to ground. Coincidence? He didn't believe in them.

"Goddamn it," he said, turning his gaze back to her, all

nice and cozy, pressed up against the man Logan hoped to do business with.

Barney laughed. "I know, she's very pretty, but don't even think about it. Nobody messes with Holstrom's women. You might as well forget her."

If only Logan could.

13

"I DON'T BELIEVE you for one second," Kensey said, looking directly into Ian Holstrom's light eyes.

"It's all true. Every last word."

She lowered her lashes, tried to fight a smile without looking as if she was having an attack of some kind. Truth was, Holstrom was interesting. No doubt about it. He was an imposing man with strong views. And he certainly understood that power was an extraordinary aphrodisiac.

It made her ill. The idea of using her sex appeal for any kind of gain was so far from who she was that it was painful.

At least talking with him was easy. Discussing art was safe, and he liked showing off how much he knew. But honestly, there was only one topic of conversation that mattered. Ian Holstrom reminded her of the sea creatures who needed to be wetted down whenever they left their habitat. For now, she was the water keeping him alive, the compliments giving him obvious pleasure, only to roll off so he required another.

"Wait, that had happened before," she said. "Steve Wynn, I think, put his elbow through Picasso's *La Rêve* just before he was to sell it to Steve Cohen for $120 million dollars."

Holstrom nodded. "One hundred and thirty-seventy million."

"He must have cursed that moment every day since."

"It was restored. And sold. I myself have purchased some of his collection. Two Gauguins. And a van Gogh."

"I'd give anything to see them," she said, her excitement real.

"Your friend Neil Patterson has outbid me on a few masterworks."

Kensey stiffened. She'd helped broker those deals, which Holstrom would know, so he was clearly testing her. "I'm aware," she said, trying to remain composed.

"I was thinking of giving him a call. To see if he wanted to change his mind."

Under his watchful gaze, she tightened her lips, briefly avoided his eyes, hoping she was sending the right signals. "He won't give me a good reference, if that's what you're after."

"I can't imagine why not. You certainly seem to know your art. You did graduate from the Istituto Superiore per la Conservazione ed il Restauro, if I'm not mistaken."

Naturally, he'd done his homework, just as she and Neil had suspected. Thank God, Sam had worked her magic. "I did. I'm an excellent curator, and my restoration work has been noted by the Met among others. Neil and I had different expectations about certain things. Personal things." She waved her hand, dismissing what she'd just said. "He's a fossil."

"That's the best description of Neil Patterson I've ever heard. He doesn't deserve the finer things in life. He certainly doesn't understand how to keep them."

She blushed. It helped the cause, of course, but she actually was embarrassed by the inference. It was all she could do not to leap to Neil's defense.

Holstrom laughed. "He's always been shortsighted, willing to spend big bucks on art, but not on someone as beautiful and talented as you." He lifted her hand and kissed the back of it. "I have to be here for at least another hour, as tedious as that sounds, but why don't we have dinner, after? We could go to O Ya."

Even she knew that was widely considered the best restaurant in Boston. She smiled. "As if we could get a table… Oh," she said. "Of course."

Amusement gleamed in his eyes. "You really have been spending too much time with Patterson."

"I suppose that's true. But, if I may be honest?"

"Of course you may."

She'd been noticing that there was an actual bubble around them. A two-foot circle where no one dared tread. Interesting. "I was hoping for something more private."

"For example…?"

"Where I could see that van Gogh and Gauguin."

The way he looked at her, she feared she'd taken things one step too far. But then he smiled. It was difficult to read what it meant, as he never seemed to lose the superior smirk.

"I'm sorry to interrupt, sir."

Kensey jumped, so used to having their sacred space. It was a young man in a suit, very deferential. Almost obsequious.

Holstrom sighed. "What is it?"

"It's regarding your trip on Saturday, sir. Mr. Siu wishes to know if you would care to stay as his guest on the afternoon of your arrival. He says you will not be disturbed by street noises."

"Tell him, no. I'll call him when I'm ready to see him.

And tell Elaine to change my booking to extend the trip an additional week."

"Yes, sir. I apologize for the interruption." The young man scurried away.

Kensey's pulse had quickened. He was leaving the country? She couldn't afford to lose ground. "Asia?"

"China. Have you been?"

"No. I haven't had the pleasure." She leaned a little closer. "My main focus of study was European art and artists. However, I'm quite familiar with Chinese art from my undergraduate years at Yale. Of course, I haven't had a reason to brush up, but I follow the auctions. It's hard to miss the names that come up regularly."

He smiled. "You mean my name."

"Among others." She was still trying to wrap her head around his departure on Saturday and what it would mean to her. It sounded as though he could be gone for two weeks, and her father could be apprehended any minute. But desperation was one of the hardest emotions to mask, so she forced every bit of it away, and thought quickly. "So, this trip, is it for Holstrom Industries business or will you be going to look at art?"

"Both. I rarely forgo the chance to see what's out there."

"No, I suppose a man such as yourself has his priorities in order," she said with a soft laugh, carefully keeping her gaze on his face. "Oh, I'm sure you've heard about the Degas that was stolen in New York last week."

There it was.

Her breath caught at the self-aggrandizing gleam in his eye. Any doubt she might've had vanished. Had she blinked she might've missed it, but he was clearly delighted by his dirty secret.

"Yes, I had heard," he said with a nod.

She hadn't planned to bring up the Degas and she hoped it wasn't a mistake. But it was all she could think of to step things up before his trip. And now she knew for certain Holstrom had the original. The trick was not to let it mess with her head. "Have you ever met Douglas Foster? Do you think he could actually be the Houdini Burglar?"

Holstrom took her arm and slowly started to move. Not clear on what he intended, her heart lurched. She'd posed a stupid question. So very, very stupid. Bringing up her father served no purpose other than to unnerve her.

"What do you think?" he asked, and her heart rate slowed as she realized he only meant to mingle. "Have you met him?"

"Once. A long time ago, but of course I know his reputation from what I've read about him."

"No," Holstrom said. "I don't believe Douglas had any part in the theft."

"I don't either, but…" Kensey lifted her shoulders in a dainty shrug. "To be honest, I'm more interested in whether Mr. Seymour is in the market for a new curator. Clearly whoever approved the security for his collection room was sloppy."

"I had the impression you wanted to freelance."

"Well, I'm not foolish," Kensey said with a small laugh. "For the right money I'd sign on with another private collector."

He smiled again, clearly pleased with her answer, just as she'd hoped. Money motivated people to do a lot of things they might not have otherwise considered moral, which was something Holstrom probably loved to exploit.

"Between you and me," he said. "I wouldn't pin any hope on Seymour. I heard he's in financial trouble."

"Really?" She drew back to stare at him. "So you think the theft is about collecting the insurance money?" She shook her head. "He could've just sold the Degas. I know of at least fifty people who would kill to own that particular work."

If she wasn't already convinced he had the original, the unmistakable gloat of victory that flashed in his eyes would have left no doubt.

"You're right, of course. Assuming the Degas wasn't a forgery."

Kensey smiled at him. "What do you know, Ian Holstrom?" She tightened her arm through his. "Tell me."

He laughed loud enough to draw some attention. "Nothing. Just speculating."

As they continued their slow walk around the room, which was suspiciously reminiscent of a royal review, they spoke of old scandals, ones she'd heard of through the years. Including some about him. "I think the first rumor I heard about you was that you had tricked an older woman, one of the Boston Brahmins, if I'm remembering correctly, out of a Monet. That her family was outraged at your manners."

Holstrom laughed at that. "That was mostly true. It's not my fault she had no idea what she was doing. If her family cared so much, they shouldn't have let her come to Sotheby's on her own. I ended up selling the piece for three times what I paid for it. I never did like that one."

She did her best to look completely besotted. "Well, you know that crowd. They pay their help below minimum wage, wring a dime out of every nickel, then expect the world to bow down to them. In my opinion, the art world needs new blood to make it vibrant. Those snooty old money people belong in their cottages, not out buying art."

"My goodness," Holstrom said, staring at her.

She hoped she hadn't just blown everything. "I know. I shouldn't say things like that. It's just…it takes money to make money, to spur creativity and make things interesting."

"Oh, I thought there was something special about you the moment I saw you."

Thank God. She could live to lie another day. In the meantime, she just walked with him for a while. He was honest-to-God nodding at people, as if they owed obeisance. A man like Holstrom didn't just steal art, he stole souls. She would love taking him down. The image of Holstrom behind bars made her smile so much more realistic.

Maybe she should go ahead and have dinner with him. Then after, convince him somehow to take her back to his place. Enough booze, and she was reasonably sure he wouldn't object. He was beginning to regard her as an ally, a confidant of sorts. Now was the time for her to act.

The trick would be not getting caught in a situation she couldn't get out of. And figuring out how to not just see the Degas, but get a picture of it on her phone. It would be difficult to prove it was the original from a photo. But if he had other pieces thought to be lost to the art world, pictures of those would help justify a warrant to search his home.

Just as she was about to bring up the topic of dinner again, his assistant, who she'd seen before, pulled him aside for a brief tête-à-tête.

She watched him carefully. Her heart sank as his expression turned deadly serious.

When he returned to her side, he was frowning, his face a dark mask compared to the one he'd worn a moment before. "I'm sorry, but I'm going to have to cut our delightful evening short. I have something that requires my attention, but perhaps I can make it up to you tomorrow night. Show you the van Gogh and the Gauguin."

"That would be wonderful," she said.

He kissed the back of her hand, and cleared a path through the crowd toward the exit.

Her heart was beating so fast, she could hardly breathe. Tomorrow night would be her only chance. He certainly wasn't going to invite her back to his home on Friday if she flubbed the job. It could save her father. Or send her to jail. And she couldn't ignore the fact that Ian fully expected sex from her.

God, what had happened to her life?

If only she could have confided in Logan. He might have helped her strategize, helped her make a plan that beat just winging it and crossing her fingers. A plan that didn't involve sex with Holstrom.

The thought of it turned her stomach.

He stopped to speak to someone else and she looked away.

Several people were looking at her. There was nothing surreptitious about it. No one seemed to mind meeting her gaze. It was as if she had gone from being a private person to a public figure, and none of the old rules applied.

She wanted out. Quickly. To talk to Neil. But she had to wait for Holstrom to actually leave the room before she made her exit. She turned back just enough to see that Ian was still there.

Please hurry.

Her desperate need to talk to Neil tightened like a noose around her neck. He could help her figure out what came next. He might have news of his own. News that would make tomorrow's dinner unnecessary. Allow her to go back to her real life. The one where she didn't think about her father. Or wear revealing clothes and have to seduce her way into the home of a monster.

She really had to get out of there. Her skin itched with strangers' stares.

She turned to check on Holstrom again. And her heart shot up to her throat.

He was almost to the door now. But what almost made her double over was the sight of another man. The man Holstrom had just passed.

It wasn't the stares of strangers that had made her skin crawl.

Logan's piercing gaze had done that all by itself.

Clearly, he'd seen her with Holstrom. And she couldn't exactly tell him the truth. But she and Logan had just managed to make a bit of headway...

She'd always known it wouldn't end well with them. Someone like Logan wouldn't think of doing what she was prepared to do, certainly not to help a man who didn't deserve it. A man who, in all probability, had sold the original Degas to Holstrom in the first place.

THE LONGER LOGAN stared at Kensey, the less he understood.

Barney was talking. Logan knew that, but it was impossible to understand the words that dripped like molasses from his mouth.

A minute ago he'd heard Barney tell him that one of the young men who trailed Holstrom was the son of the senator from Kansas. And that the beefy man walking next to Holstrom was his personal security guard.

As they neared the table, the bodyguard asked, "Have you decided what you're going to do about the blonde?"

Holstrom slapped Barney on the back as he passed by. But he didn't stop and Barney didn't say anything.

"I'm not sure yet," Holstrom said. "She might be looking for a job or a way to keep herself in designer clothes. I'll know more after I fuck her."

They both laughed, and kept walking, as if they'd been talking about the weather.

Logan wanted to punch the bastard into next week, but he held himself in check.

The rest of the world seeped into view, slowly at first, then so quickly it made him dizzy. How long had he been staring at Kensey's face? What the hell did she want from him?

"You okay there, pal?" Barney asked.

Logan looked at him. Without answering, he turned back to Kensey.

Naturally, she'd disappeared.

But then, he'd already known she was good at that.

14

Kensey closed the apartment door behind her, grateful beyond measure Logan wasn't there.

She needed to stop thinking about the look on his face after he'd seen her with Holstrom, making a spectacle of herself, and only two hours after she and Logan had had sex.

If he never spoke to her again, she wouldn't blame him. Even if she could tell him everything, she wouldn't. If he knew what she was willing to do, he'd find her repellant. Logan would probably think her father deserved to be arrested and sent to prison. So what if he'd been framed? How many paintings had he stolen? And yet she'd sell herself for him?

Oh, hell, even she didn't know how far she'd go with Holstrom. There was a chance that he'd want the fun and games to start the moment she walked into his home. He seemed like a man who'd want to cut to the chase immediately. Try out the goods before spending a whole evening with her.

Shuddering at the thought, she took a huge breath then walked through the darkened apartment, the tiles lighting her way. She'd made it halfway to her room when ⌐ front door opened and the foyer lights went on. Of course.

She really wanted to call Neil before she had to deal with Logan. On the off chance Logan didn't want to speak with her, she took another step toward her room.

"Oh, no. You don't get to run off and lock your door. Not this time. How do you know Holstrom?"

Kensey turned to face him. "What difference does it make? My relationship with him has nothing to do with you."

"Right. The fact that my future depends on contracting with HI and that you cheated on him with me?" He shook his head. "Yeah, I can see why you'd think it meant nothing. Although I've got to admit, you are a terrific actress."

"I'm not sleeping with Holstrom. I'm not interested in Holstrom. I'm—" She lowered her head, closed her eyes. She wanted to fight back. Make Logan stop thinking the worst of her.

"You're what?"

"Not what you think I am."

"What, you want to work for him since Patterson dumped you? Is that it? Great way to bypass the ladder altogether."

"No. I don't want to work for him." She managed to keep her voice steady but it was so hard to look him in the eye. "Like I said, I'm not in any way romantically or physically involved with Ian Holstrom."

"I don't give a damn who you're sleeping with. And PS, it sure as hell isn't going to be me again. The only thing I care about is getting my contract. Your game is your business, but you'd better not be screwing with mine."

Kensey had to remember that this was temporary. Tomorrow night would make or break her plan, and then she'd leave, never to see Logan again. It shouldn't have hurt her, his questions, his disdain. But it did.

She knew him well enough to believe he didn't mean

to be cruel. In fact, there'd been at least a trace of regret in his eyes before he'd averted his gaze. Which didn't, on its own, mean anything. Other than that he couldn't bear to look at her.

"Logan, I've met him twice. Both times for a reason. Someone needs my help, and while I'm not crazy about my part in making things right, I'm determined to do all I can."

She took a step toward him, grateful he didn't move back. Although he still refused to look at her.

"I guess you could say I'm trying to bring this person in from the cold. He's not dangerous. Just…" She sighed, because Logan's jaw remained tight, his body tense. "If nothing else, I'd like to think that you could empathize with that. I have no time to play nice, or to be subtle. A lot's riding on me. God knows, if there was any other way… Truth is, I'm desperate."

He finally looked at her. But it wasn't understanding she saw in his expression.

"This is a con, isn't it?" Logan said. "I doubt I'm your target. I'm not number three on the *Forbes* list of wealthiest men."

"No," she said. "No. I'm not conning anyone. Look, I didn't expect you, but when we've been together, it's been because I like you. Very much. Which is entirely inconvenient. You're a terrific guy, funny and smart and…the sex, well…that was unexpected, too." Staring into his accusing face, she felt drained. "I came to Boston to do something important, and I shouldn't have let myself get distracted. I know it's a lot to ask, but can you please trust me? Just for a little while? Soon I'll be able to tell you everything." Assuming he'd want to hear any of it. "I swear."

Her voice hadn't cracked. But now it was her turn to avoid his gaze, afraid of what she might see. How had she not realized that she desperately needed Logan's trust, even though she didn't deserve it? Or how dearly she wanted him to be on her side.

"TRUST YOU?" LOGAN SAID. "To do what? Keep playing me?"

"Please. I—"

"I'd thought, when we first met, that I'd never met another woman, not in civilian life, at least, who was as composed. As self-assured. But now I have to wonder if it was an accident, you coming out in that towel. Or if you'd been waiting for hours to spring your trap."

"No. Logan—"

"What I can't figure out is why you went to so much trouble. You could have ignored me. I'd have been fine with that. But you didn't. And now the only thing that makes any sense is that you're planning to do something to Holstrom and make me the fall guy."

Her hands were shaking. She'd flinched, but she hadn't run when he'd called her out. It would have been simpler if she had.

She reminded him too much of people he'd worked with in Afghanistan. His assets. They'd been terrified because they knew one wrong word and he'd cut them loose. And that meant they wouldn't have long to live.

Since he'd met Kensey, he'd thought about her far too often. Wondered if she really was the woman she claimed to be. It wasn't just the black ops mention. He'd thought more about that, and in truth, if she were a threat, his former CIA affiliation would've been the last thing she'd have brought up.

He tried to look at her objectively. As best he could with her standing there in that damn tight red dress. Hell. Bottom line? If she were his asset, he'd believe her. Maybe not the details, but the big picture? Yeah.

But could he trust his instincts?

Probably not. Maybe.

God, he'd gone soft. He couldn't bear watching her suffer. Standing there trying to look brave and probably hoping her legs wouldn't give out on her.

"Well, shit," he said, more to himself than to her.

In fact, she looked surprised when he approached, then wrapped her in his arms. He was surprised, too.

She curled into him, burying her face against his chest.

All he did was rub her back. As the seconds turned to minutes, he felt her muscles relax beneath his palm. Her breathing became steadier.

"I don't have a clue what to do about you," he whispered. "I know better than to let my emotions get the best of me. But something tells me you just might be telling the truth. Should I believe you, Kensey?"

She looked up at him. Her eyes were damp. Little crystals had formed on her long dark lashes. "I'm telling you the truth. As much as I can. So yes, you can believe me. But frankly, you'd probably be doing yourself a big favor by staying clear of me."

Well, he had to give her points for honesty. Unless she was playing him. Goddamn it. He wasn't this wishy-washy guy. "My sister drives me nuts trying to get me to relax. Try new things. Stop being such a damn workaholic. I think this might meet with her approval."

Kensey smiled up at him. "She sounds great."

"She is. And, I should mention, that while she's one of the most intuitive women I've ever known, she got herself into deep, deep trouble believing in someone she shouldn't have."

"Ah." She sighed. "A cautionary tale."

"For both of us." He brushed the stray wisps of hair off her face. "There's no sure way to know someone else's heart. Their true motives. All we have is our instincts. I hope you're listening to your inner voice. Mine is telling me to keep an open mind."

Kensey briefly closed her eyes. "Honestly, I'm not sure anymore. Things have gotten so complicated."

He shrugged. "Sometimes it's tricky."

Then he kissed her.

She whimpered. He doubted it was because the kiss was all that good. Although, the more he tasted her, felt her tongue tease him before she pushed his back—*good* fell ridiculously short when it came to describing how she made him feel. It seemed impossible they'd been through so much in one night. Yet they'd arrived here.

So maybe it was the truth. All of it.

Or lies. All of it.

Hard to believe that he'd fall for anyone he couldn't read.

When she pulled back, she held him still, one hand on his neck, the other framing the left side of his face. "Thank you," she whispered. "I wish this was a vacation. That I could sleep through the night and wake up feeling refreshed. That we could plot out all the fun things to do in Boston. Did you know they have food tours?"

"Wait. You mean there are more exciting things in Boston than this apartment?"

"Yep. Lots. No disrespect intended."

"I'll speak for Sam and tell you none taken. But we don't actually have to stand here all night. There are options."

She smiled. "Yes. There are."

He moved to kiss her again, and she let him, but when he started guiding her toward the bedroom, she stopped him.

"What's wrong?" Looking down at her, he could see the worry in her eyes. A place deep inside his gut sent up a flare.

"You won't say anything about me to Holstrom tomorrow, will you?" she whispered, with the same coy look she'd used on Holstrom an hour ago. For Logan's benefit, she threw in the soft doe eyes.

It wasn't just one flare now. His brain was on red alert and waiting for a KO punch. He stepped back. "That trust thing you asked me for? Remember that? My word is good. You don't need to bat your eyelashes. Or offer to trade favors with me."

She flinched. "No, I wasn't—you don't understand—"

"Oh, but I do. You can't tell me jack shit but I'm *supposed* to trust you. And keep my mouth shut." He shook his head, astonished that even now he wanted to rationalize his way back to her bed. Jesus. She was still playing him and he kept being the idiot who let her. "I've made mistakes in my life, but this one just might end up in the top five. Now I'm going to ask you a question, and I swear to God, don't even think about lying…"

"I won't." Her voice had gone small and soft. She looked miserable, but she could be thinking about the weather for all he could tell.

"Whatever the hell you have going on with Holstrom, will it impact the contract I'm trying to get?"

He knew the answer the second her shoulders slumped. If she tried to lie, he'd know it.

"It might," she said. "It's not likely, but it might."

He'd been shot before. It felt a lot like this. "I hope that whoever this person is that you're bringing *in from the cold* is worth every broken soldier who could have been helped by my company. Do you know the suicide rate for ex-military? No? Look it up."

He went to the kitchen and got himself a couple of Plinys and he didn't even slam the fridge door. Without looking back, he made it to his bedroom. He shut that one quietly, too. But he itched to knock the shit out of something.

He should have known.

Black ops for how long, and this woman turned him into an asset with one little towel. Yeah, so this wasn't going to influence his meeting tomorrow at all.

Fuck.

SHE'D WOKEN UP with a headache that wouldn't quit, and a heartache that was a hundred times worse.

It wasn't that she was in love with Logan. There hadn't been time for that. But he was in the wheelhouse. Dead center, in fact. But that was one future she'd never see. It still hurt to think he believed she would offer sex for his silence.

But then, why shouldn't he? He'd watched her brazenly flirt with Holstrom.

Damn, she couldn't afford this. Lingering over the mistakes she'd made, and then throwing out scenario after scenario about how to fix it. Always coming up empty.

She'd been up for a while. Long enough to make herself a pot of coffee and some dry toast before Logan entered the picture. With only half a pot left, she wasn't going to be any more prepared to talk to Neil. Although she'd probably find a way to alienate him, as well.

As soon as she was safe in her bedroom again, she said, "Call Neil Patterson."

A moment later, there he was, and just seeing her boss made her feel marginally better. He looked wide awake, already dressed in a gray suit, with that silk tie he'd bought in Milan.

"You look like hell," he said.

"I feel like it, too."

"What's going on?"

"Don't look so worried." She stifled a yawn. "I'm not planning on doing anything more foolish."

"More foolish? I think you'd better start at the beginning."

Clearly she should have finished the coffee before she called him. "I've got a date with Holstrom tonight," she said. "Dinner at his home."

"What happened to waiting until the final night?"

"He's leaving for China, but mostly, he asked me. I don't have any reason to believe he'd ask me on Friday. So, this is the shot I've got."

Brow furrowed, Neil didn't look convinced. Finally he said, "I don't like it."

"Frankly, I don't either. But I'm not backing out now." She looked down, and what she wouldn't give for a neck rub. "Sorry if I sounded curt."

"You're fine," he said. "But how about you tell me what's really going on?"

"The date's not enough?"

Neil's eyebrows rose.

Kensey sighed. "I said something stupid to Logan. It's got nothing to do with the plan."

"Which plan would that be? The one where you try to break into Holstrom's secret room? Because that's not going to happen. It's a fortress."

"Actually, I plan on having him open the door for me."

Neil closed his eyes for several long seconds. "I don't even want to know what you promised him for that privilege. What the hell was I thinking, suggesting you seduce that snake?"

"I've alluded. Not promised."

"He'll take first, answer questions later."

"I don't think you realize how gigantic his ego is."

"Me?" Neil leaned forward. "I don't know what about my ex–business partner?"

"You said yourself you didn't know him anymore."

"Trust me. The man's character was dubious back then, and I guarantee you success hasn't changed him into a saint. He's a louse, and he doesn't care about anything but his possessions."

"Which is why he won't—"

"Stop. Just stop. First of all, your hands are shaking."

"I'm not saying I'm not nervous. By tonight I'll have it together. You've seen me under pressure."

"Regardless, you're jumping the gun. Look, my PI is close to breaking Seymour into a pliant, cooperative witness. After Seymour met with the insurance adjuster, Phil followed him to a parking lot in Queens where he met with Detective Brown. Phil couldn't hear them, but he's got pictures and video. They argued, and Seymour was about ready to stroke out.

"Tonight, Phil's going to suggest that Seymour turn on Brown before it's too late. Seymour would not do well in prison, and Phil will make sure he believes that's only moments away. Do you see why the risk you're taking is nuts?"

Kensey swallowed. It was so tempting to back out. "I can't let this opportunity pass. I'm positive Holstrom has more pieces than the Degas. For all we know Rembrandt's *Sea of Galilee*, or Vermeer's *Concert* are in his private gallery. I can take pictures of everything."

"You're positive, huh?"

"Yes." She drew herself up straighter when she realized just how neatly she'd stepped into Neil's trap. Of course she couldn't be *positive*. "A man with that ego isn't going to waste the opportunity to show someone like me his treasure. He thinks I want a job, and that my ethics could be shaky."

"You'll end up in prison," Neil said. "Will it be worth it?"

"Thanks for the vote of confidence, boss."

"Do something for me."

A week ago she would have said, sure. Anything. But so much in her life had changed in just five short days. How was that possible?

"What's that?" she asked with caution.

"At the very least, would you please ask Logan and Sam for help? They're experts at this kind of thing, and you're not even close."

"No."

"Why not?"

"I will not involve them. And that's all I'll say about the matter."

His mouth opened, but he didn't speak. Not for a while. "Call me before you go, all right? Maybe Phil will have turned Seymour in by then."

She managed to nod before Neil disconnected.

At least she hadn't cried. That had to count for something.

15

LOGAN HAD HEARD her in the kitchen. Heard her shut her bedroom door. She probably hadn't gotten any more sleep than he'd managed. Not that he gave a shit. In fact, he hoped she'd lain awake worrying about what he might tell Holstrom.

To say he'd had a miserable night was an understatement. He tried to remember the last time he'd let such pure rage have its way with him. Definitely before he'd made it into special ops. One of the most important lessons he'd learned early and well was that anger got people killed. Over the years, he'd learned how to modify his reactions. Of course he still got angry, but a combination of mindfulness and meditation gave him the ability to emotionally disengage. Observe the situation from the outside.

He'd used every technique in the book last night, but he'd wasted his time. He kept hearing her plead with him to keep her secret from Holstrom.

Each time the words rose to the surface, or he closed his eyes and remembered that look on her face, it caught him in a vortex of fury. It didn't matter that they hadn't known each other very long, he'd given her his word.

Maybe the people Kensey hung out with made a habit of lying to her, but even that wasn't a good enough excuse.

Mostly, though, he was pissed off that she'd played him. All the way up until last night. Even after he'd caught her in the middle of whatever ruse she was involved in. He'd acted like a rookie. Worse. Like an idiot.

Right before his meeting with Holstrom.

Christ. After he'd told her all about his hopes and dreams. Although why she'd want to sabotage his efforts…

She hadn't, though. Stupidity aside, he was clear on that. He'd had a lot of time to think during the night. Kensey hadn't really offered anything for his silence. His anger had more to do with how she'd behaved with Holstrom.

Logan closed his eyes for a moment. Man, it had been tough to watch.

As far as her endgame, he couldn't come up with anything that made sense. Even last night, after he'd confronted her, she could have waited until they were having sex or right after, when he was pliable as hell before she asked for reassurance.

That would've been a smarter play. And Kensey was a smart woman.

The truth was simple and hard to take. Logan was just collateral damage. Talk about irony. It was the main reason he'd decided to leave the CIA. He'd seen too many innocents who'd been at the wrong place at the wrong time, their deaths summarized by a sad shake of the head and a rubber stamp. And he couldn't be a part of it anymore. Not even for the greater good.

He'd liked Kensey. More than he'd liked anyone in years. From that first night, she'd hooked him and reeled him in. Manipulated him until he *cared*.

Any other woman and he'd have cut his losses and moved on. But he still had half an ear out for her footsteps in the other room. The damn apartment was completely soundproof, so how messed up was that?

He took another swig of his emergency Red Bull. He would've preferred coffee, and he'd have some later. He needed the caffeine to prepare for his meeting. Barney's coaching had left Logan with some minor qualms about Holstrom, none of which were deal breakers. After he'd overheard what the bastard said about Kensey, Logan was halfway to telling Holstrom to forget it.

Which might make him feel better, but wasn't going to help many vets.

So Holstrom was a dick. It wasn't as if Logan hadn't worked with his fair share of them. He still wanted to go back to basic training and deck Sergeant Wycofsky. That asshole had been nothing but a bully. How he'd treated the fresh recruits would be illegal in any other circumstance.

Sort of how Holstrom was treating Kensey.

Shit. Logan realized he hadn't told her. He didn't owe her a damn thing, and if she wanted to jump in the shark tank, that was her problem. But he should've said something about what he'd overheard.

He shoved thoughts of her aside and got out of bed. He wanted to make himself a pot of coffee, but he didn't want to cross paths with her.

He stopped. What the hell was he thinking? He wasn't about to tiptoe through the last couple of days. If she had a problem with that? Tough.

As he settled down with his morning cereal and coffee, he reviewed his talking points for the meeting. Every time he found himself thinking of Kensey, or worse, coming up with reasons not to meet with Holstrom, he pulled himself back together.

After the second hour, he barely thought of her anymore. Not even to wonder if she was hiding in her room.

He doubted it. More likely she was out somewhere, stirring up more trouble.

Not ten minutes later, the doorbell surprised him. He glanced at the digital peephole viewer and immediately opened the door. "What are you doing here?"

"Now that's the kind of welcome that makes a person feel all warm and fuzzy," Sam said, stepping into the foyer. "I'm glad I caught you."

She was supposed to be at the exhibition hall getting ready to wow the crowd with her newest invention. She certainly looked dressed for the part. "What's wrong?" he asked. "Don't you have somewhere important to be? Like showing off at your booth?"

She smiled as she walked past him. "It's pretty funny when the big suits come by. They all nod as if they know what I'm talking about, but an hour later their tech guys ride to the rescue." She went straight to the kitchen and stared at the coffeepot.

"How old is that coffee?"

"A couple hours, give or take. I can make a fresh—"

"That's okay. I'll take a Pliny."

"Seriously?" He glanced at his watch. It was ten-thirty.

"One beer won't kill me."

Something prickled the back of his neck. Screw it. He fetched them both bottles. His meeting wasn't for a while. "What's going on, Sam?"

She took the beer, and instead of sitting down in the living room, she led him to his bedroom. When the door was shut behind him, he turned again to his friend.

Sam drew in a deep breath. "I think Kensey might be in trouble."

Every muscle in Logan's body tensed as he immediately went into fight-or-flight response. He grabbed the doorknob.

"Whoa. Hold on," Sam said, catching his arm. "Not

right this instant." She pulled him away from the door. "I meant tonight."

"Shit, Sam. I hear the word trouble from you, and I don't know what to think." He took a moment to settle down. "But if this is Kensey's tactic to get me to help her, it's not gonna happen. She made her bed. I'm not interested in who she sleeps with in it."

Sam looked down at the area rug, and Logan's gaze followed. His bottle of Pliny was by his feet, sideways, the beer still gurgling out.

He picked it up, then went to the bathroom. Not just to get a towel, but to save some face. He hadn't realized that he'd cleared his dominant hand in preparation for pulling out his weapon.

When he returned, Sam was perched on the end of the bed in her floaty wide-legged pants. She didn't pay any attention to his mop-up.

"Kensey doesn't know I'm here," Sam said.

"Be careful of her. I know you trust Patterson, but he probably doesn't know what she's up to, either."

"Yes, I do trust Neil. And he believes Kensey's about to get in over her head and isn't thinking clearly."

"She seemed pretty goddamn assured last night."

"I gather she did something to piss you off, but that's probably because she's desperate." Sam studied him. "Though you can't be that pissed. You almost pulled the door off the hinges trying to get to her a minute ago."

"It's just reflex," he muttered.

"Whatever you say, hotshot." Sam shrugged. "I can't tell you much, but I do know that there's a good possibility Holstrom has a collection of stolen artwork at his estate that has tighter security than my lab. Not just art, either. We're talking Mona Lisa art. Masterpieces that should be in museums. Rembrandt, Matisse, Degas. No one has ever been able to prove that he's got them, and that's what Kensey is trying to do."

Logan shook his head. Sam could be absentminded. And she was what someone might call dense at times, but overall she was crazy smart, so what the hell? "Do you hear what you're saying? It's possible Holstrom, not just any Joe Blow, but *billionaire* Ian Holstrom is in possession of stolen artwork. No one has ever been able to prove it. But Kensey is gonna charge in and do that all by herself?"

"Pretty much," Sam said, nodding. "So you see why she needs our help."

"Jesus." Logan scrubbed his face. "I'm going to wake up any minute and all this nightmare bullshit is going to disappear."

"Nope. I don't think so. Not unless you agree to help."

He watched her take a sip of her Pliny. Most of his had been soaked up by a towel. It pissed him off all over again. "She told me she's trying to save some mysterious person who's in danger. She can't even keep her story straight."

Sam shook her head, her red hair flowing over her shoulders, her gaze bright with intent. "That's not true. From what Neil told me, I'm guessing an innocent person is being accused of stealing an important piece. That's grand larceny on an epic scale. And that's why Kensey has to prove that Holstrom has it."

"Shit. She's just the kind of idiot who would try something that stupid. How does she even know that Holstrom—no. Don't tell me. I don't want to know." He stretched his stiff neck muscles. "If I were you, I'd try to talk her out of it. If you can't, then walk away, because whether Holstrom is guilty or not, he has the kind of money and power to make sure anyone involved with Kensey is going to pay dearly.

"Hell, I'll probably end up in jail just for sharing the apartment with her. And may I just compliment you and

Neil and your friend Kensey for making it nearly impossible for me to walk into my meeting today without prejudice."

"You need prejudice. He's a horrible thief."

"Allegedly."

"I think even Neil believes Holstrom is dirty."

"Then he should call the police." Logan didn't blame Sam. He understood she felt she owed Neil, but she wasn't thinking clearly herself. "Look, if I knew Holstrom was crooked, then yeah, I'd take a step back. But since that remains an unknown, his money can help a lot of people. So right now, I don't care who signs the checks. I care about my company, and the good it can do."

"Huh." Sam stared at him with the head tilt he hated. "I get it. I do. Your dream is hugely important and of course you're entitled to do what you like. But Neil's going to help Kensey, and so am I. I'm a little disappointed that you aren't helping, too."

"That's just perfect. Icing on the cake. Now that woman is coming between you and me."

"She's not. Your decisions are based on something I don't know about, so I'm absolutely not judging you."

"You just said—"

"Fine. I'm judging you a little. But only because you're my hero. That's not your problem, either."

"That's nice, Sam. I mean it. But I missed that mark by a mile." He cleared his throat, wishing he'd gotten another beer. "Out of curiosity, has she tried calling the police? Seems like that would be something they'd be interested in."

"Not without proof. Like you said, it's Ian Holstrom." Sam frowned. "I talked to Kensey a few times before I met her in person, and she's not an idiot or stupid. How do you know you're not the one who's wrong?"

"Oh, so now you don't trust me, either. Jesus, Sam."

"I never—"

"You know what, it's fine. I basically disappeared for ten years. That's a long time, and we've both changed. It hasn't been easy to be my friend. Hell, when I finally did become a civilian…" He exhaled, needing to get his bearings. He wasn't used to this kind of talk. "That first year was messed up. I—"

"Logan. Stop. Please."

"No, I'm just saying I haven't given you a lot to go on. We've revisited the old days, but I don't think we've caught up. The truth is I've done plenty of things I didn't agree with, for people I didn't like. Because it was my job."

He turned away, finding it hard to meet Sam's eyes. They'd never discussed the mission that had motivated his decision to leave the CIA, and they never would. Never could. It didn't matter. All his skills, all the superior training he'd received had failed him that day and he'd learned to live with it. But he could make up for it now.

"I need Holstrom's money," he said. "But the truth is, I could get money elsewhere. Holstrom has corporate and government contacts it would take me years to make on my own. But as a subcontractor, I'll be granted credibility just for being under Holstrom's umbrella.

"I know what good I can do with it. So don't ask me to join in Kensey's scheme. A lot's at stake and there are repercussions to everything, Sam. Everything."

Sam got up, walked over to him and threw her arms around his neck. He jerked in surprise first, then held on tight to her, too. They didn't say anything for a long while, and he was glad of it because it gave his racing heart a chance to slow down.

"I'm sorry if you think I don't believe in you," Sam said, pulling back to look into his eyes. "I do. You're a superhero, and always have been. And you're my friend.

So knock him dead, Logan. Get all the money you need from him to make your company great."

"Good advice. Now go back to your booth and shake up that place. And try not to worry about Kensey. Holstrom's place must be a fortress. She'll never even get inside."

Sam kissed him on the cheek, then headed for the door. "Kensey won't have to break in," she said, looking back with a small smile. "She has a dinner date with Holstrom tonight. At his place."

"I ADMIRE YOUR work ethic," Holstrom said, watching Logan like a hawk, ready to pounce as soon as Logan missed his footing. "So what is it exactly that you think I can do for you by subcontracting your company?"

"I think we both know the answer to that." They were ten minutes into the meeting. It felt more like an hour. "The real question is what I can do for you. Besides solidify your presence on foreign soil."

Holstrom's slow patronizing smile told Logan that he had about three seconds to show he wasn't bluffing. "Money, you have. But that's not all you want. I can make you look good. Show everyone you're the sort of patriot the public just loves to place on a pedestal.

"Not only will you get the kind of publicity that makes for big awards ceremonies, but I'm also involved with three different international veterans' organizations, and I'll make sure you're on each board of directors. All without you having to do much more than pose for the covers of the *American Legion Magazine*, circulation 2,284,729. *VFW Magazine*, circulation 1,264,347, *Family*, circulation 501,543, *Airman*, 500,000, *G.I. Jobs*, 360,000. I can go on."

"I'm sure you can, Mr. McCabe. How much money will this venture of yours cost?"

Logan had no qualms when he doubled his already inflated fees. Holstrom didn't even look too surprised. If he had reacted negatively, Logan wouldn't have cared. No way this egotistical asshole was going to talk him down, not when Logan was dangling a very important missing piece in Holstrom's portfolio.

Barney had given Logan a lot to go on with Holstrom, but Logan had done some poking around himself. The goodwill of the armed forces was important to the man, and there was no way Holstrom hadn't figured out Logan's CIA connections. Logan may not have the lesser government contacts he needed to expand, but he did have access to the highest echelons of power. In fact, he'd thrown out his entire playbook the moment he'd seen Holstrom. He really disliked the sleazy bastard.

Every time he opened his mouth it reminded Logan of those obscene words the prick had said about Kensey. Not that Logan was changing his mind about helping her. But just imagining her entering the lion's den tonight made it very easy to push hard and take no prisoners. Manipulating Holstrom was a piece of cake, now that Logan knew what to look for. And if or when Holstrom offered him the contract, Logan didn't have to take it.

"If I were to bring you into the fold, I would want you only for foreign security business. Nothing domestic."

"Well, that's a problem," Logan said, lounging back in the leather guest chair and noting the irritation in the man's face. "Granted, most of the vets I employ excel at operations on foreign soil. But not all of them want to go back to the Middle East or be sent to South America, certainly not for any extended periods of time. I'll need the ability to offer them some assignments right here at home."

Holstrom tightened his mouth but he didn't say anything. Yesterday Logan would've been pleased with the grudging admiration in the man's eye. Today he didn't give a shit what Holstrom thought of him or his spiel.

Goddamn Kensey. Though he should thank her. This new attitude was working in his favor.

They went back and forth for another hour, and by the time Holstrom's lackey du jour had come in twice to remind his boss he had other obligations, Logan had everything but the signed papers. It was still difficult to shake the man's hand.

As soon as he got out of Holstrom's booth, he called his sister. He'd asked her to dig deep, using every connection she had to find out more about Holstrom and his relationship with the art world.

He'd been so busy doing the same for Kensey, he'd almost been late to his meeting. But more and more pieces of a puzzle he hadn't known how to solve were becoming clear.

Her stellar reputation identifying forgeries had been confirmed in enough ways that Logan was convinced it was true. And so were her boarding school years. In fact, there were a lot more avenues to follow once he was back at the apartment.

He wasn't about to let anyone pull his strings again. But now that he'd been dragged into this mess, he was determined to discover the truth about the woman and her mission. He rarely used his own special resources. The Big Guns, as Lisa called them. Still, it was nice to have friends in the army and the CIA. He had a few more in the NSA, but something told him not to invite anyone there to start probing into Kensey's life.

Damn her. Why couldn't he shake this ridiculous need to protect her?

16

KENSEY STARED AT her reflection and saw a stranger. How had she gotten here? What on earth was she doing?

Ian Holstrom expected to have sex with her. Because she'd made him believe it was what she wanted, too. She doubted very much that he was the kind of man to live by the "no means no" rule. Or any rules, for that matter.

She closed her eyes and pictured what her father would look like behind bars. Each time she imagined him there, which was far too often, it was a little bit worse. She may not succeed with her plan, but if he was in prison, at least she'd be able to go see him.

It wasn't as if she loved him. She didn't know him. The father she'd loved would never have walked out on her. So tonight she'd better think things through before Holstrom's car arrived. Was all this worth pleasing the idea of a father? One who would explain everything. Who would have the best reason ever for abandoning his daughter? Not that she believed in fairy tales.

But she desperately wanted to believe in the one.

Make that two. In the second tale, Logan would forgive her, and they'd get together in New York when all of this was over. She'd cook dinner for them. Or they'd meet at the coffee bar down the street from her office. And they'd make out on a bench in Central Park, alarming the Tai Chi gang and the pigeons.

Yep. That was the dream. In reality, she might find herself in a hell of a lot of trouble tonight.

Maybe she should just tell Holstrom straight out that she had black belts in two different martial arts. But that wouldn't get her into the secret room. No, she'd have to play her part, and play it well.

She checked the time. The car wouldn't arrive for an hour and a half. Holstrom called it a car, but that was just billionaire speak for limo. Like the mansions in Newport being called cottages. She knew from her research that he lived on a large estate. Even though it might have raised some red flags, she should have insisted on taking a cab. But she wasn't fooling herself either. Taxi or not, he could make it difficult for her to leave before he collected on her unspoken promise.

Nothing about Holstrom led her to believe he was a gentleman when it came to women. But if he pushed too hard, well, she had a few tricks up her sleeve.

Anyway, knowing Neil, he'd probably be tracking her movements from the moment she stepped outside the apartment door. Even if she were taken to a place other than Holstrom's residence, she could always send out a text SOS. It sounded gross, but she knew a woman who had gotten out of a frightening situation by barfing on her attacker's shoes. That maneuver might shut things down real quick. And she wouldn't have to physically hurt him.

She slipped her robe on over her underwear and took three outfits from the closet. They were the final contenders and she laid them on her bed. Taking a few steps back, she stared at each one, imagining what it would be like for him to see her for the first time.

Of course she imagined Logan first. That was a recurring theme. She'd try to focus on Ian Holstrom, but Logan always barged in on her thoughts. It was taking a lot of numbing concentration to stay on point.

The first outfit was a cream-colored formfitting dress with dolman sleeve and an off-the-shoulder neckline. But it was tight all the way down to the hem past her knees. If things got rough, she'd have a difficult time.

Next was a sheer, floral-print silk charmeuse blouse with skinny pants. Wearing an outfit like that, she'd have no problem defending herself, but even with a flesh-colored tank, the see-through fabric made it look as though she was naked underneath. It was very sexy, and she wasn't sure she wanted to be that obvious.

The last choice was the simplest: a pale pink cashmere pullover hemmed at the waist with suede skinny pants.

All three had pluses and minuses, but she'd go with the pullover, and save the others for another time. To wear for someone she wanted to be with.

Damn, why did she have to keep torturing herself by thinking about Logan?

His meeting would be over by now. She wondered if he'd gotten the contract. She wouldn't ask even if she had the opportunity.

She needed to stay focused on tonight, mentally prepare herself for any possible outcome. To that end, she'd found a well-reviewed beauty salon not too far from the apartment. She'd had her hair done, a spa mani-pedi and a half-hour chair massage.

None of which had relaxed her for more than ten minutes, not even the massage. Hardly a surprise, considering she'd used the time to think about Logan. And fret over how badly she'd bungled things with him last night.

Shaking her head, she picked up her cell phone and checked it for the tenth time. It was her only ticket to taking the pictures she needed, that is, if her nerves didn't do her in first. She doubted Holstrom would welcome a selfie with her and the stolen Degas.

A noise from the living room stilled her. She'd heard Logan come home about ten minutes ago, and she was reasonably sure he'd either go out again or stay in his room until she'd left. Luckily, she had no need to leave her bedroom until the car arrived.

The knock on her door set her heart racing. Guilt washed through her, as if she'd robbed the Met or something.

The second she opened the door he barged right past her.

"Okay," he said, his voice as stern as a ruler across knuckles. "This is how we're going to play it."

Without so much as a glance at her, he dropped a paper bag on the bed, next to her clothes. When he finally turned toward her, he had clasped his hands behind his back and stood tall, his feet shoulder length apart. For the first time she could truly see the military in him.

He looked hot as hell. Damn him.

"Play what?" she asked, matching his curtness. "What are you even doing here?"

He didn't answer her immediately, which pissed her off.

"Well?" she asked at the same time he said, "Your dinner with Holstrom."

Something new ignited inside her. And it wasn't lust. There was only one way Logan could know about her dinner. Neil had gone behind her back.

The betrayal hit deep and hard. The only man she'd ever truly trusted since her father had deserted her was Neil. And he'd done what she'd very clearly asked him not to. She wished Logan would leave. She wished she'd never come to Boston. She should have let her father do whatever the hell he wanted, and forgotten about him the way he'd forgotten about her.

But she sucked it up, found her anger and let that fill the hole in her gut.

Then waited until she was reasonably sure her voice would hold up. "Neil?"

Logan stared back at her without speaking. Something dark and primal flickered in his eyes before he closed himself off to her.

"So, Neil called Sam, and Sam called you, and now you've decided to ride your white horse into my business. Well, you're not welcome. Get out."

"You're right. That is how I found out about your plan. Or perhaps we should call it something else because a plan has a chance of succeeding."

"Oh, get the hell out of my room." She pulled the door open wider, as if that would make him budge. But he really needed to go. Despite her very real anger, the sadness and betrayal made her want to cry, and she wasn't going to cry in front of him.

That it was *Neil* who'd betrayed her was almost inconceivable. She couldn't blame Sam, although scratch that potential friendship. And of course, Logan. The way he was looking at her made everything a hundred times worse because she couldn't read him.

From now on, she'd take her chances on being alone. She'd still work with Neil, but it would only be work.

And if Logan wasn't out of there in the next minute, she was going to make sure he would walk out limping. "If I'm such a loser, what are you doing here?"

"You want to get rid of me? Call off this idiotic mission that could land you in jail. Or worse."

"What do you care, anyway?"

"I don't," he said without as much as a blink. "But Sam does. And I care about her."

Kensey's chest ached, right where his verbal punch had landed. She kept her expression as impassive as his. "Nobody needs to worry about me. Now, go."

"You don't even know if he has the stolen masterpieces."

"Logan, please. If you really do care about Sam, you have to leave me alone. It's critical I stay focused. You understand that like no one else does."

Concern briefly shadowed his face. "I'm going to wire you up so I'll be able to hear what's going on between you and Holstrom. I'll be close enough to step in if things go FUBAR."

"Wire me up? Are you crazy? The man must have metal detectors or whatever latest device there is to find out if he's being bugged."

"And we have Sam," he said. "She's come up with something that hasn't reached the open market yet. The wire will be undetectable, and you'll be able to use it for cause to get a warrant."

Dammit, he had a point.

She had to get some air into her lungs. The way he spoke to her as if they'd never met, let alone made love was making her ill. Another deep breath and she said, "I don't know if we're going to his estate or somewhere else. He's sending a car. If I am going to his home, it's got to be guarded like Fort Knox. No way he's not taking every precaution."

"Thanks for the heads-up, but it's not my first rodeo, and you don't have the kind of time you need to run through every scenario you can think of. I'm ex-military special ops. When I say the wire isn't a problem, it isn't a problem."

"Go to hell, you smug bastard."

"Whether I'm smug or not, I'm still going to save your ass," he said. "For Sam's sake."

"You've made that quite clear." She looked down, hoping she hadn't given anything away. Yes, she was hurt. But not over him. It was Neil's betrayal that stung. "I appreciate your concern for Sam. I do. I like her, too. But I've got this."

"Fine. Tell me your plan. If I can see its merits, I'll stand down, no sweat."

Tears threatened again, but she fought. Hard. "It isn't a plan so much as a launching pad. I'll go to his place, and I'll play nice and ask him to show me his private collection. The way he wants into my pants? He'll cooperate."

"And…?"

"I'll have to play it by ear."

Logan's head dropped back so he was looking up at the ceiling. The goddamn colors of the walls kept getting darker and darker and she wanted it all to just stop.

"Oh, for Christ's sake," Logan said. "Play it by ear?"

"I'm not as naive as you think. And I know how to take care of myself. I've got two black belts. He tries anything, he'll lose a hand. Or something else."

"You still don't get it. You are absolutely that naive. And by that I mean you are headed into a world of trouble, and you don't even know it."

"I know his ego is so large it barely fits through doors, and he wants to show off. Especially to someone like me who knows art. The one thing about having a secret collection is that you can't brag about it."

"He didn't get to where he is by being an idiot."

"No," she said. "But he is a man. And he doesn't suspect me to be anything but a gold digger with an advanced degree. He'll want to share his secret with me, because I'm going to be sufficiently interesting to him."

Kensey saw Logan's jaw tighten.

"I'm not really going to sleep with him."

Their eyes met dead on. She almost wished she couldn't

see the turmoil in his gaze. He'd been stone cold so far. What had changed? Why now? Maybe he did care a little about what happened to her. Despite being a stubborn ass, he was, in the end, a good man. One she might have had a chance with.

Just because that was water under the bridge, it didn't mean she'd stopped caring about him.

"You do realize," she said softly, the fire and indignation gone from her voice, "that if you're implicated in any of this, you'll be finished. Not just with Holstrom, either. You're risking your reputation and your vets."

His jaw flexed, but he didn't respond.

"How did your meeting go?"

Anger blazed in his hazel eyes. Didn't he understand she wasn't taunting him? She only wanted him to see reason.

"Look," she said. "The person I'm trying to help was framed, but he's not an innocent man. Get it? He's not someone you'd cross the street for. And if things do go badly with Holstrom, I should be the only person to suffer the consequences. Please, please just drop it. Walk away."

A great huff of air widened his nostrils, but he didn't crack. Or leave. Instead, he moved closer to her. "I'm going to tell you something…" He paused, clenched his jaw. "At the reception, after I saw you, Holstrom and his toady left the room. As he passed my table I overheard him say that he didn't know what he was going to do with you yet, but he'd figure it out after he fucked you. Is that plain enough? Do you see what and who you're facing?"

Her stomach roiled. She felt dizzy for a moment, and luckily, from where she was standing she was able to steady herself against the armoire.

Logan took another step toward her. And though his expression remained as tight as a waxworks doll, she could tell he'd been ready to catch her if she fell. More important, she knew what that one step meant.

"That's…not surprising, really," she said, firmly on her own two feet once more. "But thank you for telling me. I can handle him."

He stared at her, his expression one of complete disbelief. "Do you honestly think I can ignore what that asshole said and leave you to *play it by ear*?"

"Logan, please," she said, after what felt like a ten-minute pause. "I don't want you involved. Maybe I was foolish for not asking for help sooner. Okay, not just maybe. I admit it… I was foolish. If I'd reached out, perhaps I'd have a better plan that wouldn't have the potential to blow up in my face. That doesn't mean you and your vets should get caught in the explosion."

No response. Just hard eyes and tight mouth.

"For what it's worth, if you won the contract, I wouldn't blame you for being happy, even though it's Holstrom's money. You'll do good things with it. That counts for a lot. That's why I'm asking, begging you to walk away."

Even that didn't move him.

She just wished she didn't still want him so much.

"Are you even listening?" she whispered, starting to feel unsure again. She understood the risk was huge and everything was stacked against her, but she'd never wanted anyone else to be dragged into this with her.

"*You* need to do the listening," Logan said, all business. "This wire could save your life. It's made with a material Sam created, that no software or hardware can detect. You're the first person to use this outside of beta testers."

Kensey blinked at the thing Logan was holding. It looked like a chewed piece of gum and about the same size, only it had a string attached.

"It comes with an earpiece that is very small, and very powerful. Nothing will be able to detect that, either. Secondly," Logan said, as he reached into the paper bag, "you're going to wear these bracelets."

They were pretty. Very slim, silvery and slinky, and they would complement the outfit she'd selected, but why would Sam lend her jewelry?

"Only two matter, and for this demonstration, we'll be looking at this one," he said, showing her the bracelet that had a slim green thread snaking around it. The others also had threads like it, each a different color. "If you get inside the secret room, this will be your camera. All you have to do is drop it. Which is easy to do. The catch has a little bump where the others don't."

He put the bauble in her hand, and she was able to find the bump easily.

"Now put them all on. The green one last."

She did. They looked perfectly natural on her arm.

"All right. Now press the bump."

It took less than three seconds to find it and press. The bracelet somehow lost its gleam, and if she hadn't been looking straight down at it, she'd never have seen it at all. It didn't even make a sound on the hardwood floor.

"Watch, now. Pay close attention. It's difficult to see this part."

Following his lead, she crouched down, not blinking for fear of missing whatever she was supposed to see. There. It was flat, like a snake. Then the tiny front of what she would have sworn was liquid, rose a tiny bit. Maybe a sixteenth of an inch before it started turning. The whole thing. And with each turn, it moved forward. The head was always higher than the body, but nearly translucent.

"What's it doing?"

"Taking pictures. Thousands of them, three hundred and sixty degrees, every surface in every light condition. If the room goes dark, the tech running the base unit, from miles away, will turn on infrared, which can be decoded on the base computer. That will be with me. It happens at lightning speed and it will only stop taking pictures when either the computer sends it a signal or it hits the farthest wall. That could be the end if the room is small, but if it's large, the camera will continue in a different direction, like a Roomba vacuum, until everything's mapped. It will also stop if it's picked up. So be careful not to drop it too soon."

She finally looked up. "This is magic. This is beyond anything I've ever heard of. How do the images look?"

"Sam's example was Blue-ray is 1280x720. This baby is 15360x8640."

"Oh, my God."

Logan stood and so did she.

"Sam was going to debut this tech today. Instead she's letting you use it."

"Can't she debut it, as well?" Kensey asked, and he shook his head. "I can't take this. It's too much."

"She'll insist. That's who Sam is," Logan said.

When Kensey tried to launch another protest, he held up his hand. "We can't afford to waste any more time."

She just nodded, humbled at Sam's kindness. The device was a godsend. It would make Kensey's job so much safer and simpler.

"Let's talk about distress calls," Logan said. "We have to decide on words or phrases you can use to let me know you need help. For example, if you were to say, 'It's gotten awfully warm in here,' I would know it's time for me to rush in."

"No." She stared at him. "You can't ever do that. No matter what happens, Holstrom can't know you're involved."

Logan sighed, giving her a look that indicated he thought she was being naive again.

"Promise me you won't."

He dismissed her with a cold, hard stare. "We'll go

with 'It's awfully warm in here,'" he said. "And if you just want to let me know that you have eyes on the paintings, then—"

She quit listening. All she needed to do was get the proof, and leave without ever tipping her hand. She'd be damned if she'd allow Logan to come running in to save her. He'd watched her yoga routine. But maybe he really didn't get that she was very good at defending herself if the need arose.

"Now, take off the robe."

She blinked at him. "What did you say?"

He was holding the wire again. "The robe," he said, gesturing.

Even though he'd seen her naked, she was still uncomfortable taking the robe off. She had on a very small thong because of the pants, and a matching sexy bra, one that she'd bought for the purpose of seduction, just in case…

He touched her shoulder. She gasped as if he'd burned her, but he touched her again, this time on the side of her breast. The device itself was very slim. But it had to be pressed against her skin like a bandage. The place he chose was just below the cup of her skimpy bra.

He leaned in, and she smelled his favorite shampoo. The one that smelled like a forest. Her heartbeat accelerated and she knew he could feel the way her breath caught with every brush of his fingers. God, his breath across her skin gave her goose bumps.

Logan cleared his throat. A sign he wasn't having an easy time of this, either?

She straightened her posture and fixed her gaze on the wall behind him. Then she began reciting multiplication tables in her head.

He froze, and lifted his head a few inches. Oh, God. She'd leaned into him. Without being aware. Her right hand was halfway to his chest.

Aflame with embarrassment, she pulled back. But when she looked down, she could see the bulge behind his fly.

It seemed so cruel to make them so attracted to each other when nothing could come of it. She wondered if it would matter that the other reason she didn't want his help was because she might be falling in love with him.

17

GODDAMN HIS BODY. Traitorous thing, no morals whatsoever. All he was doing was affixing the wire to Kensey's bra. He couldn't help thinking about the perfect curves underneath, the softness of her skin and how he knew exactly how her nipple tasted.

In fact, he should be mulling over the excitement on Kensey's face when she'd realized what the bracelet camera could do. She'd had no qualms about his involvement now that Sam had made her incredibly stupid plan incrementally less dangerous. But still stupid.

And he was halfway to a full erection.

He was thirty-three, not thirteen.

Maybe he was turned on by his confusion. One minute he was certain she was completely sincere about keeping him removed for the sake of his veterans. Trying to do the right thing. That she was in over her head and genuinely didn't want to involve him.

The next minute, she didn't seem to give a shit about anyone else. Including Sam, whose sacrifice was stunning, considering how many sales she could have made from debuting her camera to the security crowd.

The only thing pushing him toward the more favorable view was Sam's conviction and her trust in Neil Patterson. Logan had a suspicion, though, that Sam would have gone to the mat for Kensey even if Neil hadn't asked.

He'd also seen the devastation on Kensey's face when she realized the only person in the world whom she had trusted completely had gone behind her back. Her shock and loss hit Logan in a surprisingly visceral way. He should have been pleased that she'd experienced what it was like to have her own trust thrown in her face. But he wasn't. Which wasn't to say he'd forgiven her, or had come to trust her. But he also knew Neil had been completely justified in his concern that Kensey could be in serious trouble.

She'd headed toward this night with blinders on. His chest hurt when he thought about her walking into Holstrom's lair without a plan. Going in his car. Jesus.

Logan had to stop trying to make sense of this woman. He wanted her. He liked her. He'd hoped to see her once they returned to New York. But she'd made that impossible. Which was all the more reason for him to stay away from her.

He reached the end of the small wire, but he was reluctant to move his hand from where it brushed against her breast. Was he nuts?

Wrenching himself away, he retrieved the incredibly tiny earpiece. Sam had assured him that all he needed to do was place it behind her ear, in the fold. It wouldn't be noticed there and it wouldn't fall off.

"Hold still," he said, moving Kensey's hair behind her shoulder. Her scent was stronger there. It was the mix of her shampoo, the one that smelled like the ocean, along with the too-well remembered smell of her skin. He'd liked kissing her where her shoulder met her neck, and it had never failed to make her tremble.

His eyes opened, and he hadn't remembered closing them. Before he could make a horrible mistake, he pressed the tiny device exactly where Sam had said to, then stepped back, turning quickly. Kensey didn't need to see him in this state. It would be completely misleading.

He wished he could just walk away now. But none of these high-tech gadgets meant Kensey would be safe if things got ugly. She thought she could take care of herself and Logan understood why. In most scenarios she could probably kick ass. But between Holstrom's ego and power, if things went sideways, Kensey didn't stand a chance.

"Thank you."

Turning only his head, he met her gaze. "For what?"

Kensey blinked at him. "Everything."

"You should get dressed," he said, turning away again. "What time will the car be here?"

"In thirty minutes."

"Good. Don't take too long. We'll need to test the equipment before you leave. I'll be—" He pointed his chin toward the door.

"Fine. I'll let you know when I'm dressed."

"It'll take me about ten minutes to get everything working and to turn on the mic. After that, walk around, talk, open and close doors. Basically, don't be afraid to make noises. I need to figure out the mic's limits."

"Okay."

He left, the empty paper bag crushed in his fist.

He'd kill for a scotch. But he'd settle for a beer. What he grabbed from the fridge was a soda.

Once he was in his room he opened his laptop and, using Sam's software, he studied the test pictures the green snake had taken. They were better than any HD shots he'd ever seen. When the images of Kensey came through, he saved four of them directly to his desktop. Three seconds later, he realized what he'd done and sighed. If he had half a brain left, he'd delete those pictures immediately. After tonight was over he needed to regroup, concentrate solely on his work. And forget Kensey.

From the checking he'd done, he was fairly sure the man she was trying to help was Douglas Foster. Logan couldn't prove it, but he was reasonably certain Foster was Kensey's father. The Swiss boarding school she'd told him about checked out, but when she hadn't been in attendance, she'd remained in Europe the same time Foster was staying in his French villa. Her extensive knowledge of art was a big indicator, as well, and her age was right. Those were too many coincidences for his taste.

Then there was Neil Patterson. He'd stepped in as the perfect parental surrogate. Logan wondered how much he knew about Foster. Kensey herself had said the person she was trying to help wasn't innocent.

What a damn mess. In every way possible.

And still Logan wanted to wrap her in his arms and pretend the rest of the world didn't exist. Not forever. Just for a little while. Wanting her was purely physical. He'd get over it.

He checked his watch and wondered if she was about ready to test the mic. He put in his earpiece, figuring she'd let him know when it was time.

Tonight was going to be a bitch. Listening to her talking and laughing with Holstrom. If Logan was right about Foster—and he was 90 percent certain that he was onto something—it was no wonder Kensey felt the need to keep her guard up. He'd be a hypocrite to condemn her for that, given the years he'd told his family and friends so many lies of omission it had felt like treason.

Even so, he was unable to let go of his anger and his disappointment. Anger that was probably too large for the offense, but he couldn't shake it. Disappointment not in her, but in the truth he'd finally seen. They had too much

baggage to be together. Trust would be an issue. He still
couldn't erase her stricken look when she learned Neil had
betrayed her confidence. And Patterson was her closest
friend and ally. How would they get past that?

Logan cursed his own stupidity. They weren't his problem. Kensey wasn't his problem. Not after tonight. He had
enough on his plate. More than enough. After all this shit
was over he'd be back to looking for someone else with
deep pockets and great connections.

"Logan? Can you hear me?" Her soft voice felt like
a caress.

"Yes."

"What would you like me to say?"

He closed his eyes.

Nothing. Not one damn thing.

It was too late.

KENSEY STEPPED OUT of the limo and smiled at the driver.
Holstrom's Tudor-style mansion reminded her of boarding school. The home was nearly as large, the surround-
ing landscape lush with beds of roses and trellises with
green, climbing vines.

She walked through the stone courtyard to the front
entryway, wondering where her host was. A beep too
loud to be anything but an alarm sent her straight toward
cardiac arrest.

"Don't mind that." Ian Holstrom appeared as if the
beep had summoned him. "These days, you can't be too
careful." He held out his hand. "All it means is that you
don't have any weapons and aren't carrying any bugs."

"Ah," she said, letting him lead her into the house. "I
imagine someone in your position needs to take extra
measures."

He smiled. "May I?"

"Oh." Kensey realized he was asking for her purse.

Her phone was inside so she hated handing it over to him but she had no choice.

She took in the expanse of what was basically the foyer. Except it was huge. Bigger than most Manhattan apartments. Everywhere she looked, there was something ostentatious. Gold leaf on the mirror? Check. Enormous crystal chandelier? Check. She watched as he laid her purse on an intricately carved antique console table.

Then she was pulled into an embrace that tested every ounce of discipline she had. It wasn't bad enough that she hated being constrained by him, but when he pulled back only to kiss her, she put on the show of a lifetime.

It was so tempting to bite the tongue testing the seam of her lips. Thankfully, her moan of distress sounded more like something it wasn't. Yes, Sam's "accessories" were a godsend and could mean Kensey's success, but knowing that Logan was listening to everything was pure torture.

How had she ever thought she could do this?

Holstrom finally let her go. "What can I get you to drink? I have an excellent wine cellar. Are you familiar with Harlan Estate?"

"Yes." She didn't have to fake her surprise. A bottle could go for five hundred dollars. "I certainly wouldn't ask you to open something that expensive."

He smiled as he leaned against her side. "But you wouldn't turn it down if I brought one up, would you?"

She suppressed a shudder at the feel of his breath near her ear. "You know me too well."

"Kindred spirits, eh?"

"Well, if my being dazzled by the fact that you've got a Chagall over your fireplace is any indication, then yes. May I get closer, or is the guard I saw outside going to run in and slap my wrist?"

"Bruno? He watches the gate. I have another man monitoring the camera feeds. That's all I need. This place is locked tight."

"Does that mean I'm free to…?" She swept a longing glance at the Chagall, hoping Logan caught that bit about the camera feeds and stayed put.

"Of course." Ian gestured her forward. "We'll save the wine for dinner. How about a drink for now?"

"Yes, thanks. A vodka tonic, please? Not too strong. I don't want to miss a thing in this amazing house…is that a Whistler?" She nodded to one of the paintings on the far wall. "*Little Arthur*?"

She'd hit a bull's-eye with that one. It was from Whistler's early years. Not one of his most famous works, but still a surprise to see on a wall that wasn't in a museum. When she got close to the Chagall she stopped acting. It was gorgeous. A piece she'd never seen in person, but she knew it had been sold to a private collector.

Ian brought her drink, but she could barely look away. When she told him the provenance of the painting, she'd expected him to be impressed. Not breathe heavily in her ear. As she walked around the expansive living room, he preened like a peacock when she got things right. There wasn't a single painting she didn't recognize. And she pretended not to hear when he delayed dinner.

Finally, there was nothing else to fawn over, and he pulled her into another kiss, this one far more intimate. Behind her closed eyes, she pretended it was Logan, but Holstrom missed the mark by a mile.

He led her to the formal dining room. She'd so hoped they'd be at the head and tail, but no, he was at the head and she was at his side. The first thing she did when he took his seat was touch his thigh. Quickly. Then she turned her attention to a silver setting on a sideboard.

"Is that…?"

"Yes?"

"It can't be. That was marked as lost almost a hundred years ago."

"Really?" A hint of a smile tugged at his mouth. "What do you think it is?"

"A tea service made by Paul Revere. I'd say in the 1780s. But...?"

Ian raised one eyebrow. "Of course not. How would I get my hands on an original Revere tea set?" Then he winked.

Her heart leaped. Good. He was letting her slip into his private world. She put her hand just below her necklace. "Well, this evening should be very interesting."

He smiled and then ordered a bottle of the Harlan Estate Napa Valley Bordeaux blend from a maid wearing the traditional black-and-white uniform.

The first course came moments later. Lobster bisque, liberally dosed with dry sherry and garnished with truffles. Although she'd had better, she said otherwise, because she couldn't go wrong with a compliment. Ian really was a flattery hog.

Despite the privilege of tasting the fantastic wine, the rest of the meal continued in the same manner. It was almost unbearable to know that Logan heard every word. He must be going crazy out there. Not from jealousy, she no longer believed that was possible, but from the inanities of the conversation. She'd attempted three times to speak of something that didn't revolve around Ian's perfect taste, and failed each time.

There was one exception. She'd told him about the Modigliani that Neil had in his Tarrytown office. How it was one of the lesser works, but she didn't expect Neil to know that since he lacked good taste. She'd rolled her eyes, and Holstrom beamed with pleasure.

When they finally finished the meal, he dismissed the household staff. Which made her nervous. She couldn't react, though. All she could do, really, was continue to play her part. And stop drinking anything but water.

Ian took her hand as they walked through the living room.

"I can't believe I'll have to go back to New York the day after tomorrow," she said as they entered a long hall-way. "Boston has so much to recommend it."

"Such as?"

"Art collections?" she said, as coyly as she could when they stopped in front of another stunning piece. "That's John Francis Murphy. I've only heard of two paintings of his in private collections."

"They're both mine."

She let out a reverent sigh. "I'm a huge fan of Tonal-ism. I've seen several by Inness, and of course, Whistler, but this…it's amazing."

"I have more," he said.

She inhaled as if she'd been offered the Whistler as a parting gift and looked at him with admiration.

"You'll like the regular collection," he said, his eyes narrowing just enough for her to see the test for what it was. Surely he wasn't normally this obvious. He wanted her to win this contest.

She deflated a tiny bit. Then brought her smile up as if she'd placed second in the Miss America contest.

He laughed out loud. "You are a greedy little thing, aren't you?"

"Why not want the best of life? We're only here for a short time, after all. What good is having the finest crys-tal if it never holds champagne?"

"What good indeed." He stepped very close and put his hand on her shoulder, his fingers sneaking under the material of her cashmere top.

"I'll show you mine," she said.

He smiled.

"After you show me yours."

He acted affronted, but he let his hand move down to cover her breast. "After, huh?"

"I'd be ever so grateful."

"Yes, you will." He pulled her into a bruising kiss.

She kissed him back because, God, she was so close. Now wasn't the time to lose her nerve.

After what seemed like an eternity, he pulled back. With his arm around her waist, he led her to a private elevator. They went down two floors, and when the doors opened, she could see the only thing that mattered. It was a door protected by three kinds of security precautions. Retinal scanner, fingerprint recognition and voice recognition.

Kensey made a comment about a collection that was robbed using a 3-D printer. Then she laughed. "It was their own fault. Most places have fingerprint and retinal scanners, but adding the voice recognition like you did would have made it exponentially more difficult to exploit. Kudos to you."

Then the door, as massive as the one at her bank, swung slowly open as Kensey held her breath.

18

Logan was on high alert.

The feeling was old in his bones. It had been honed by years of listening for details and watching in the dark. But tonight was different because Ian Holstrom was getting ready to do something very, very bad.

Logan had known from the moment the staff had been dismissed that the night wouldn't end well for at least one of them. Preferably, Holstrom, but Logan knew better than to count his chickens.

The equipment at hand was the best he'd ever used. These past couple of years Sam's work had taken a quantum leap. He knew for a fact that she'd been wooed by governments and big corporations who promised her the moon and the stars, but she'd said no. Good for her.

He checked his tablet and watched the green dot go from the dining room and through the living room. The wire under Kensey's bra was also a tracker. His attention was split between listening to the conversation and never letting the tablet out of his sight. Things could change in a heartbeat.

Goddamn, this was a stupid waste. Yes, he understood that the paintings, if they were there, belonged to the world, but it shouldn't have been Kensey saving them. If she and Patterson believed this strongly that Holstrom was guilty, there were trained agents who could have done the job. Sure, he knew she could take care of herself. She was strong, superbly fit. But he also knew how soft her skin was. How easily breached.

Every five minutes he'd had to squelch the urge to run inside and give Holstrom a good beating. He'd promised Sam he would do all he could to keep Kensey safe. But not to interfere unless it was absolutely necessary.

He'd heard Holstrom kiss her. Heard the moan that he assumed meant she liked it.

Logan knew better.

Holstrom was a rich man with power. The kind who thought he could do anything at all. That nothing could touch him.

Logan knew better about that, as well.

When Holstrom had taken her purse, Logan had started using his relaxation techniques. It was tough, though. He kept slipping back to red brain, allowing stress chemicals to take over and interfere with logical, calm thought. Kensey talking about her precious artwork had relaxed him back to green brain. Not that he couldn't think in the red, but he preferred strategizing when he was calm, then going on the offensive while he was steeped in fight mode.

Holstrom laughed so loud it hurt Logan's ear. "You are a greedy little thing, aren't you?"

"Why not want the best of life? We're only here for a short time, after all. What good is having the finest crystal if it never holds champagne?"

"What good indeed."

Logan took another deep breath. He didn't know what was happening, except that Holstrom's loud voice meant he was practically on top of Kensey.

"I'll show you mine," she said.

Logan clenched his fists.

The quiet was making him insane. He stood, tablet in hand, earpiece on, and started pacing.

"After you show me yours."

Luckily, that had been Kensey's gambit, not Holstrom's. Letting out some pent-up air, Logan pictured exactly how he was going to get into the estate, then into the house. Sam to the rescue again. He'd be virtually invisible unless he bumped into one of the two guards on duty, but he'd been following their patterns since he'd pulled the van into a copse of thick evergreens just outside the grounds. The man stationed at the gate rarely left his small enclosure. Probably reading or watching TV. The other guard was probably checking the monitors and didn't realize he had a pattern. One that would be incredibly helpful. Every thirty minutes he left his post to have a smoke with his buddy in the booth.

Logan also knew how to bypass the front door alarm. His Glock was at the ready, but he wouldn't use it unless Kensey's life was in danger.

"After, huh?"

Every word that bastard said put Logan's hackles up.

"I'd be ever so grateful."

"Goddamn it, Kensey. Don't even—"

"Yes, you will."

"Over my dead body." Logan winced. Thankfully, Kensey wasn't able to hear him. She wouldn't, unless something urgent came up and he adjusted her earpiece to send and receive.

Christ, more kissing.

It was getting harder by the minute to think of doing business with that asshole. The money and connections would have meant so much, but the idea of putting the top tier of the United States armed services and Ian Holstrom together now chafed.

He had to believe that there was some other way to raise the money. As for connections, he wasn't out of the loop. He just didn't have a track record in the private sector to justify getting the juicier contracts. Still, he'd find another way.

He stopped pacing to watch what had to be an elevator going down. After a moment, Kensey told him exactly what he could expect at that lower level. On such short notice, he'd never make it inside the room, so if Holstrom closed that door with Kensey inside, she'd be on her own.

Shit.

Logan didn't like that scenario. Not one bit. He waited as long as he could, then decided he had to assume the worst. He'd already figured out how to avoid the cameras, but he still had the guards to consider.

He strapped his tablet into a holster that he'd rigged earlier and made sure the computer was ready to accept any input from the snake Kensey was going to release. Then he set his stopwatch for two minutes, nine seconds, which was when he'd be in the clear to scale the iron gates. He'd have four minutes, forty-eight seconds to get inside the home without being seen by security. From there, he'd go down the emergency stairwell to the bottom floor. That was when he'd turn Kensey's ear receiver on.

This was fight mode, and this, too, was part of his DNA. God help Holstrom if he touched her…

KENSEY GASPED WHEN she felt Ian behind her, putting something over her eyes.

"Don't be afraid," he said, his voice so close she could feel his breath. "Trust me. You'll like this next bit."

It was all she could do not to elbow him in the stomach, then take him down like the pervert he was, before he realized what was happening. Then she'd take off the blindfold. That was the only way she would *"like this next bit."*

He propelled her forward, her hands out in front of her because the bright light of the secret room was now an afterimage that would take a while to disappear once he took the blindfold off.

And why the blindfold in the first place? As she took her next tentative step, she remembered all too well what Logan had overheard. The second she could be sure they were inside the room, she would *accidentally* elbow Ian and use that moment to both release the camera and take the thing off her eyes.

The way he was breathing told her that his fondest wish would be to screw her while looking at his stolen treasures.

"Just another few seconds," he said.

She didn't wait. Her elbow went back. She heard his *umph* as she spun around, and ripped off the blindfold, which was actually his silk tie. "Oh, my God, I'm so sorry," she said, quickly dropping the bracelet. "Did I hurt you? Is there something I can do?"

She knew she'd hit him hard enough in the diaphragm to wind him. The satisfaction of seeing his red face gasping for air was pleasurable in the extreme. Not that she showed it. Concern was all he would see as she made anxious noises.

"I didn't realize you were so close," she said, remembering a bit late that she didn't want Logan running in. "But don't worry. I must have hit the wrong spot and made your diaphragm spasm. You'll get your breath back in a minute, I swear."

It took longer than a minute. But finally, he was upright and not pleased with her at all. She could see he wanted to punish her, and the only thing she could think to do was turn around to the showroom and gasp at the first picture she saw. "It can't be, can it?" She looked behind her, all innocence and wonder, before turning back. "That's *Waterloo Bridge*. The Monet. It was supposed to have been burnt by the thief's mother."

He chuckled, moved closer to her. One look at him, and she could tell he wanted this part of the evening like a junkie wanted heroin. She was his perfect audience. Someone who could actually understand the breadth of his collection.

"Oh, no," she said, not having to fake her earnest disbelief. "You have both of them? The *Charing Cross Bridge*, too? I can't even imagine what they'd go for at Christie's."

She started moving faster, anxious to find the Degas among the labyrinth of paintings. The room was large, possibly half the length of his house. And set up a great deal like the Metropolitan Museum in New York. The extensive collection of pieces he'd hoarded was staggering, all properly lit and framed, the temperature and humidity of the room perfectly calibrated. Whoever had built this room understood the care of fine art, and how easy it was for moisture to damage them.

"You have the entire Rotterdam collection?"

"You tell me," he said.

She moved to the next work, laughing at the sheer joy of seeing that Lucian Freud, and Meijer de Haan's self portrait hadn't been destroyed.

She stopped. Couldn't have moved for anything when she saw Picasso's *Tête d'Arlequin*. Tears came to her eyes, but also, a lot of anger. This unbelievable bastard was worse than she'd ever imagined. When she looked toward the back wall, she saw it. The missing Degas. The original.

"So you like my little collection, eh?"

Holstrom had moved directly behind her, and his hands clamped around her arms, holding them tight against her body. "I knew you would. You're a little art whore, aren't you?"

Here was the punishment she'd earned by her trick.

He kissed her neck. Then bit her. Just enough for her to cry out. "I am," she said. "And I want the same thing you do, but I have to see the rest. Please. I'm desperate to see everything."

The way he squeezed her arms would leave bruises. But instead of giving in to the urge to pull away, she stood her ground and moaned as if she wanted him to hurt her.

"I'll guide you. After all, I know what you like."

She just nodded obediently and the pressure on her arms relaxed, but not by much. "Now, what's this one?"

"Henri Matisse. *La Liseuse en Blanc et Jaune.*"

Holstrom let go of her arms. "If you're a good girl, I'll let you see more," he whispered. "I want you to put your hands behind your back. Don't move them until I tell you. You don't need hands to look, do you?"

"No," she said. "Of course not. It's fine." The last bit was for Logan, certainly not the sadist in back of her. She obeyed, hating him more than she'd ever hated anyone. Still, she kept her eyes reverent, her voice submissive. She had to be sure the camera had enough time to do its job. If Logan barged in now...

Oh, God.

"You've kept them in perfect condition," she said, then sent Logan another message. "It's smart to have me put my hands behind my back. I'd never forgive myself if I accidently touched one of these masterpieces. I can't even imagine what they're worth. Millions."

"Millions?" Ian laughed. "Turn around."

She did. His hands went to her wrists this time. Holding them with the intent to bruise.

"Close your eyes. I'll tell you when to open them."

Of course, she obeyed. He moved her forward, then turned her and stopped.

"You may open your eyes now."

Again, she gasped. No wonder he'd laughed when she said millions. She was looking at something she thought she'd never see in her lifetime. "That's Rembrandt. That's *Rembrandt. Storm on the Sea of Galilee.* It's so…"

He laughed again, but she didn't care. No matter what happened to her, she had to get these paintings away from this madman. His right hand moved, and she felt it under her sweater. Moving up until he reached her bra. He found a way to tuck the top part of her cup under her bra so her breast was completely exposed.

She wondered if he'd just broken the contact she had with Logan. But then she shifted her entire focus to the painting…on the brushstrokes, and shading. No one had bettered Rembrandt even after all these years.

Holstrom teased her nipple. "Tell me what you know."

She held in a curse. "It was painted in 1633. Stolen on the morning of March 18th, 1990, from the Isabella Stewart Gardner Museum by thieves dressed like policemen."

"Very good," he said, then he squeezed her nipple so hard she couldn't hold back a shocked cry. She wanted to tell Logan to wait. That she was fine. Maybe it was for the best if the wire had stopped working.

Finally, Holstrom let go, and she breathed again. He took her down the row of eleven other stolen or "destroyed" pieces, and she told him about each one. But he didn't hurt her, except when he reclaimed her wrists. At least his sick game was keeping him occupied. Letting the camera snake do its work.

Finally, he stopped her in front of the Degas. Her breath escaped her in a whoosh and her legs got a bit wobbly. Not just because this would prove her father didn't steal it, but because she didn't know if he was the one who'd stolen it in the first place.

Holstrom's right hand left her wrist and before she could catch her breath again, she felt it on her inner thigh.

There weren't that many paintings left. As soon as they were out of this room, she would have him on his damn knees.

Just as his hand was inches away from her crotch, she heard Logan.

"Don't move."

It wasn't coming from the earpiece. He was in the room with them.

"Except for that hand of yours," Logan said. "Unless you don't mind losing it."

"What the hell… McCabe?" The hand disappeared from her thigh, but the other was still on her wrist, squeezing hard. Holstrom stared at Logan as if he were seeing a ghost. His gaze swung briefly to her, before returning to Logan. "What are you going to do, shoot me?" he asked. "There are priceless works of art in here."

"I know a really good art restorer. I'm sure she could do wonders."

Holstrom grunted, and released her.

She spun around. Logan's eyes were both wild with fury and so in control it was chilling. "Get out of here, Kensey."

"We all have to get out of here. But, if he doesn't co-operate, please shoot him in the knees, using a downward trajectory. That way the paintings will only have mini-mal damage."

"What the hell is this?" Holstrom didn't sound so smug anymore.

"This," Kensey said, "is where we leave the room." She let Logan usher Holstrom out, while she walked around until she found the camera snake. It was moving back toward the door, but not on the same side as the Degas. She hoped it had already gotten the right picture, but she couldn't tell.

Taking a final look around at all the breathtakingly exquisite paintings, she wished she could do something to ensure Holstrom went to jail for this crime against humanity, but she couldn't. Not now, at least. She picked up the bracelet and put it back on her wrist. The pictures might provide grounds for a warrant, but Holstrom would have moved every last painting before the ink was dry. But she'd known that coming into this mess.

When she joined the men outside the room, Holstrom, hands still up, was glaring at Logan, his face red with fury. "I gave you a goddamned contract, you bastard. For three times what your lousy company is worth."

"Yeah, about that... I've changed my mind," Logan said calmly. "Kensey, do me a favor. Take this gun. Feel free to shoot him anywhere. The spatter won't matter out here."

Holstrom didn't move a muscle during the transfer, though it felt great to point the weapon at him. But before she could truly enjoy the feeling of power, Logan landed a punch so hard, Holstrom hit the floor like a discarded rag. A second later, Logan pulled him up by his tailored shirt, just to hit him again.

"Logan," she said, fearing he wasn't nearly done. "Enough."

He didn't look at her. His gaze never left Holstrom's face as the man struggled to stand up again. Kensey wasn't sure if Logan had heard her. He looked like nothing could stop him. A frisson ran down her spine. Earlier she'd seen his military side, but this was the warrior. Terrifying and hot as hell.

"Go ahead, rough me up," Holstrom said, wiping the blood from the corner of his mouth. "It'll look good when the police get here and I explain how you broke in and tried to kill me."

"Sure, let's call them." Logan took the gun. "I'm sure they'd enjoy a viewing of your private collection, too."

Fury settled in Ian's shrewd eyes. "You honestly think I'd do one day in jail? No judge in this state would deny me bail. As for your precious military, you think they'd let me be put away? They come crawling to me for weapons," he said, looking at Logan. "You shouldn't have hooked up with this con artist. Because I'm going to make sure there isn't one person on earth who will fund your pet project. I won't quit until you're homeless. You understand me?"

Logan's smile turned predatory. Dangerous. "No matter what, you won't come out of this smelling like a rose, Holstrom. I promise you that. The stolen artwork aside, you assaulted Kensey."

"As if anyone would take her word over mine."

"They don't have to. We've got everything on tape. Can you imagine, Kensey, what all his customers would think if the details were leaked? I bet he wouldn't be getting any more humanitarian awards. In fact, you know what? I'd love to have an extra souvenir." He reached with his free hand into his pocket and pulled out his cell phone. "Why don't you go take a picture? I don't care what painting it is. You choose. We'll wait here."

She didn't think twice, just took his phone.

"Hold up," Logan said before she took another step. "I think I'd like me and my buddy to be in the shot. Just a small insurance—I meant to say memento of our visit." He grabbed Holstrom by the collar. "What do you say, Ian?"

"Fuck you."

"Logan?" Kensey didn't give a damn that she heard Holstrom's shirt tear but it was risky to go near the art again. "Let's not—"

Logan's warning look silenced her.

She moved aside, then followed him to the back of the room where she watched him position Holstrom next to the Degas. Then Logan pulled something out of his back pocket. He unfolded the front page of today's paper and held it up in front of him.

He gave her a nod. "Okay, Ian, say cheese."

She took the shot, the scope of Logan's cleverness slowly sinking into her poor muddled brain. The picture, establishing today's date, probably wouldn't stand up in court, but there was a good chance it could be used to clear her father. Her hands shook a bit, so she snapped a second shot for good measure.

As soon as they were out of the room again, she put his phone back into his pocket.

"Well, guess we'd better be going," he said. "Not that we haven't enjoyed your hospitality."

Holstrom looked at her, then at Logan before he put his hands down. His lip and left cheek were already swelling. "Why the hurry? You know, there's a deal to be made here. I'm sure you two didn't go to all this trouble just to walk away with nothing to show for it."

"Thanks for the offer," Logan said and glanced at his watch. "Maybe next time."

"Here," she said, handing him the tie Holstrom had used to blindfold her. "Maybe you can make a knot that won't take him *all* night to get out of."

"My pleasure," he said, passing her the Glock.

Kensey wanted so much to just take the Rembrandt. Arrange for it to mysteriously appear at the door of the Museum of Fine Arts. Weirdly, almost as though he knew what she was thinking, Logan gave a small shake of his head.

She wouldn't have taken it, anyway. The risk for damage was too great. At least when Holstrom moved everything, which he absolutely would do, he'd take good care of the paintings. He might be a sadistic prick, but he was too greedy to cause them any harm.

Of course, she thought of just calling the police. Since Holstrom was restrained, he'd be caught red-handed. But she couldn't see his guards allowing anyone, not even the police, onto the estate without Holstrom giving the okay.

They were armed and they'd come looking for him, and she refused to risk a shootout with Logan. She'd just trust Neil to help get Holstrom later.

Getting out was relatively easy. She found her purse on the table where Ian had put it. They waited until the timing was right and—hidden from any electronic alarms and security cameras—they ran for it.

Thankfully, Logan's rental van wasn't too far away. It finally hit her that it was over. She'd found what she'd been looking for. And just as he unlocked the passenger door, she realized she was still shaking, only harder now. "Logan."

He stopped, looked at her.

"Where are the guards?" she asked. "There were two men…"

"I didn't hurt them if that's what you're thinking. My guess is they're about ten minutes away from finding Holstrom."

"How do you know that?"

"His security system is set up with some kind of fail-safe signal tied to the lower floor access and probably other parts of the house. If it times out, the guards would automatically do a check." Logan shrugged. "I don't know for sure but that's what I would do. That's why he tried to stall us at the end. You okay?"

She nodded, leaning against the side of the van. "I want you to know I was ready to take him down myself so you wouldn't have to get involved. I really was. I never wanted you to lose anything on my account. I'm so, so sorry."

"You're trembling."

She felt just a bit lightheaded but she'd be all right once she sat down. "I hope you believe me," she said, as her vision got narrower and narrower.

Suddenly, his arms were around her, holding her close. She might have lost a few moments there, but now she relaxed in the comfort and safety of his arms, even if it was temporary.

It couldn't last forever, though. "Thanks," she said, taking a step back. "I'm fine, really." She looked up, hoping he might kiss her.

"Good." He let her go, opened the passenger door and walked to the driver's side.

Kensey prayed he could see now that she'd told him as much as she could, that she'd never once tried to trick him. "You know I had nothing to do with Neil calling Sam, don't you? I expressly asked him not to tell anyone."

Logan's response was to start the engine and get them onto the main road. "I'm glad you're all right," he said finally. "And I hope you got what you needed."

"I hope so, too," she said, so softly he probably didn't even hear.

"I couldn't have worked for him," Logan said. "He's a real snake and I'm sorry he touched you. I wish I could have stopped that..." His mouth tightened. "No sense rehashing things. We're done now. I'll return everything to Sam, then catch the first flight out to La Guardia."

They were done now?

She looked at his strong profile. At the way his jaw was set, his gaze on the road and nothing else.

He didn't mean they were just done with Holstrom. Logan meant the two of them were over.

19

"WE'VE HAD THIS argument before," Logan said, wanting to strangle his sister. Normally they got along great, but sometimes... "You know what? Forget it. I'll take this case. You can have tomorrow off. You deserve it after doing so much when I was gone."

Lisa sat up straight. Only a moment ago, she'd flopped down on the chair across from his desk as if she'd been too exhausted to hold her head up. "I was kidding."

His gaze went to the big calendar he kept on his office wall. How could nine days have gone by since he'd returned home? "It doesn't matter. Take the day—"

"Logan, stop. Jesus. I was just trying to lighten the mood. Frankly, it's getting scary. You're not yourself."

"That's got to be an improvement."

"Maybe if you'd just talk to someone..."

He looked at his inbox. It was so full he wanted to run away from home. "You're right to hate these stupid divorce cases." He huffed a laugh. "If I hadn't screwed up in Boston—"

"Oh, for God's sake. You really need to stop this right now. You didn't screw up. You did the right thing."

Lisa didn't understand. He'd screwed up, all right. Not

just the deal with Holstrom. He'd messed up everything with Kensey, too. All that anger and disappointment that had consumed him? Turned out it had little to do with her. She was a civilian, doing the best she could to help her father. Logan had blamed her for her perfectly logical weaknesses. She was an art curator, not a trained spy. And the way he'd treated her...inexcusable.

Despite the years he'd spent back on United States soil as a civilian, the therapy he'd gone through, the appearance of being all right with the world, he'd been holding on to some wicked judgments about his last mission. He should have taken the shot. That was his job, and he'd disobeyed an order. Why they'd wanted to refuse his resignation was still a mystery.

And he'd done it again in Boston. He'd had a single goal: to get what he needed to expand his company and hire more vets. He'd failed. It didn't matter that his personal moral code made Holstrom problematic. He should have signed the contract that same day.

The deal might've fallen through anyway, since Holstrom was arrested five days ago, thanks to Patterson rallying some high-ranking judges who happened to be avid art collectors. But that wasn't the point.

Logan had put Kensey first. She was one person. That he'd fallen in love with her shouldn't have entered the picture. The veterans he could have helped had come in a distant second.

And given the choice to do it all over again, he'd have done the same thing. He'd have protected Kensey if it had meant losing everything he had.

He knew better. He'd been trained to see the greater good.

And in some crazy, weird way, the Boston fiasco had somehow given him the closure he hadn't realized he needed. Because he could honestly say, despite not knowing the repercussion of his decision to stand down in Afghanistan, he'd have made that same choice again, too.

He'd stayed as long as he could, and he meant no disrespect, but the war had caught up to him. He'd seen too much. Too many innocent people had died, and he simply couldn't take it anymore.

Logan wished it hadn't taken ruining his chances with Kensey for him to see that his choices had been true to his code of ethics. Part of him believed that was all he could hope to do in this life. Stand true to himself, no matter the cost. The other part of him, the loyal soldier, didn't believe it for a minute.

It seemed he and Kensey had both ended up collateral damage.

"Hello?"

Lisa was leaning over his desk. "First of all, you know you couldn't have gotten in bed with Holstrom. Can you imagine what your vets would have thought of your judgment?"

He swallowed at his sister's unfortunate turn of phrase.

"Second, have you called Kensey? She might not hate you, you know."

He wasn't going to argue about this again. Luckily, the office phone rang. They both reached for it at the same time, but he won. "McCabe Security."

"Hey, it's me."

"Hold on a second, Sam. Lisa's here. I'll put you on speaker." He pressed the button. "What's up? Something wrong with the order I sent you?"

"Have you called Kensey?"

He dove for the button to take Sam off speaker, but his sister got there first. "No," she said. "He hasn't. Because he's being an idiot."

"Shut up." Logan considered yanking out the phone cord. "Both of you. It's not your business."

"It is if you keep moping," Lisa said.

"Please, Logan," Sam pleaded. "If you'd just call her—"

"Look who's talking, Sam," he said. "Really? You want to go there?"

"Okay. If even I can tell you guys are meant for each other—"

"This isn't why you called. Or if it is, I'm hanging up."

"Fine. Have you been keeping up with what's going on with Holstrom? He's being excoriated by the press."

"I know most of the paintings were confiscated as they were being prepared for transport," Logan said. The arrogant prick had figured he had more time before a warrant would be served, assuming there was a judge with the balls to issue a warrant in the first place. "I was hoping he'd had the three missing pieces on the jet when they picked him up trying to board. I spoke with Neil yesterday, but he didn't say. You know anything more?"

"No," Sam said. "I didn't know you guys were in contact."

"Yeah," he said. "I've agreed to testify if need be, but we're trying to keep Kensey's name from coming up. Not officially. And it's really thanks to you, Sam. You saved our collective asses. I can't ever repay you."

"You can."

Logan winced, knowing what was coming. Sam gave him a phone number. One he'd already memorized but hadn't found the courage to use.

Kensey closed Neil's office door behind her and turned without moving toward her usual chair. "He called," she said.

"Which one? Your father or McCabe?"

What Neil just asked should have offended her, but she couldn't rally her anger. "My father. He called. He's in New Jersey. He's been there the whole time."

Her boss put down a file and relaxed back into his big leather chair. "And?"

"He'd read in the papers that Seymour and Detective Brown had been arrested. The warrant for him is gone."

Neil smiled. "You must be happy about that. It's what you wanted all along."

She wasn't about to keep leaning against the door like some waif in a Dickens novel. But she didn't want to sit down, either. She moved to the window and stared down at Central Park. "I am," she said. "But he wants to see me."

"I'm not surprised. Are you?"

"Yes. He's been to New York before without sending so much as a text. Why should this time be different?"

"Maybe he feels he might have more to lose?"

Kensey turned around. "Well, that wouldn't be far off the mark. He's a thief, after all. One I helped set free."

"But he wasn't guilty. Not of that crime."

Kensey sighed. "I'm still not sure why I did it. Or why any of you helped me. I was a menace. The risk wasn't worth the reward. I don't suddenly feel like forgiving him. He's been a bastard."

Neil nodded. "He's aware."

She wasn't sure she was prepared for this conversation. "Excuse me?"

"He also called me."

"Why?"

"Because he desperately wants to see you. And he wants to find a way to make reparations without going to prison. He thought I might be able to help."

"You shouldn't. This is all on him. You've already done too much."

"I wouldn't really be helping him."

She turned to the window, not that she could see anything with her eyes filling with tears. Again. Nine days had gone by, and she was still a mess.

"I want to see him," she said. "But I don't know if I want to see the man he is now. Maybe I should just stick to the memories. I have a different family now." Her voice barely came out a whisper. She'd never said it out loud before. It had been true for a while, at least with Neil, and now she had other people she cared about.

Kensey felt reasonably sure Sam was someone she could count on. Who Kensey would do anything for. The only glitch was that Sam kept calling, trying to convince her to get in touch with Logan.

Logan, who hated her, but had put his ass on the line for her, anyway. He'd lost so much because of her, which was made infinitely worse by the fact that she was desperately in love with him. She'd tried to deny it, but that didn't lessen her pain.

"I've waited too long to say this to you," she said. "Thank you. So much."

"You've said it at least a dozen times since you returned."

"Not for going against my wishes, I haven't." She walked over to his desk. It was beautiful, like the one in Tarrytown, only this one was more elegant. It went with the rest of his huge office. All rich wood, gorgeous bookshelves filled with leather-clad tomes he'd actually read. Needless to say, the artwork was stunning. But none of that mattered more than his friendship.

"I was furious with you. And disappointed. It took me a while, but I know that everything you did, you did because you care about me. And you recognized that I wasn't thinking clearly. You're more than I deserve."

"Not true at all. I'm exactly what you deserve."

She smiled.

"Have you said that to Logan?"

Her spirits spiraled like a windless kite. "No."

"You should. He risked a lot."

She nodded. "I know. I wish a lot of things were different, but involving him, and you and Sam, that wasn't fair. I hope I never do anything so foolish again."

"I assure you, if the circumstance calls for it, we'll be there. Now, about your father?" Neil waited calmly. It was one of his best and worst traits. "You deserve the truth," he said when she remained quiet. "Whatever it turns out to be."

Her phone rang. It was Sam. Kensey hesitated.

"Go ahead," Neil said. "I have a teleconference anyway."

"Hi, Sam." Kensey headed for her own enclave a few doors down. Her shelves were stocked with books on art, so many that she'd lost count ages ago. She skirted her tidy desk, and settled in her overstuffed chair. "Good timing."

"Great." Sam sounded too cheerful. "What did Logan say when you spoke to him?"

"Very tricky," Kensey said. "I haven't called him. He hasn't called me."

"You're both idiots. And I'm not talking about your IQs, although they might come into play if you don't do something. Tell me you don't miss him like crazy."

"That's the problem. I do. But he hates me. He told me flat-out we were done, and then he never looked at me again." The tears came, though not the subtle kind like earlier. She started bawling like a baby.

"Oh, God," Sam said. "Please don't cry. This is why I like computers. They never cry. I don't know what to say to you. So, you can't do this all the time. I feel completely helpless, but I really want to be your friend. Just tell me what to do."

Kensey sniffed. "I don't know. I've never had friends. Or been in love." There. She'd said it out loud.

"About time you admitted it."

She grabbed a tissue. Just in case. "This is all new to me. I want your friendship, too. You're amazing, and you're funny and sweet. I owe you, big time."

"You mean that?"

"Of course I do."

"Then call him. Please. You're both so close to getting this right. You trusted me for other things, now I'm asking you to trust me as your friend. Call him."

Kensey closed her eyes. If Sam was right it would change everything. But if she was wrong, Kensey's world would shatter. Living in limbo certainly wasn't doing her any favors. "Fine. I will. I'll call him."

"Now."

"No. It's bad enough I just cried hysterically. I have an appointment in thirty minutes."

"Then when?"

Sam really wasn't letting up. "Tonight. From home. Okay?"

"Promise?"

"Yes."

"Cool. If you like me now, you're gonna love me later."

Kensey smiled. "We'll see. I've got to go. I have mascara all over my face."

It was almost seven, and Kensey was still pacing. She'd made a salad for dinner but ended up opening a bottle of wine and just having that. She was on her second glass, and she was still jumpy and fearful. What had happened to her calm, cool exterior? She'd perfected the walls around her for ten years, and in four days they'd crumbled.

No wonder she'd never fallen in love before. It was horrible. A nightmare. God, how did people survive this?

Another sip of wine and she got all the way to the counter, where she'd put her phone. She reached for the damn thing, and nearly jumped out of her skin at the knock on the door. Damn. Stella. Her neighbor had threatened to come by but Kensey had forgotten. When she opened the door, it wasn't Stella.

"Hey, uh," Logan said, "is this an okay time? I know I should've called…"

She nearly tripped on her own feet scrambling back to let him in. He looked gorgeous, tall and lean in dark jeans and a gray Henley. She was still in the black sheath dress she'd worn to work. He crossed the threshold and her heart fairly beat out of her chest.

Eventually, she shut the door, while he was still checking out her place. The co-op was huge for New York. The open-plan kitchen and living room made it look even bigger.

"This is great," he said, and she heard his nervousness despite the blood rushing past her ears. It shocked her. Why would he be…

"Not really surprised about the art on your walls, and I do like your taste. For the most part."

"Yeah?" She almost wept with the way he'd steered the conversation to something comfortable, at least for her. "Which part doesn't do it for you?"

"This one," he said, motioning to the Rothko print. "It's just stripes."

"If you don't feel it, you don't. It speaks to me."

Logan turned. "I'd ask you what it says, but I'd like to speak to you first." He winced, but she didn't think she was supposed to have seen that. Again, he'd calmed her down at his expense. Or maybe she was reading too much into things.

"I wanted to call you." She felt her face heat, the wish for a happy ending so strong it was difficult to think. "Wine?"

"Sure."

Halfway to her fridge, she stopped and looked back at

him. The way he was staring at her stole her breath. "I have beer. It's not Pliny, but it's from a local brewery."

His grin was like the one in her dreams. "Now you're talking."

She gave him his beer, and topped off her glass, amazed she hadn't spilled anything. They moved to the living room and she offered him the couch. She took the chair directly opposite.

"I'm sorry," he said.

Confused and a little alarmed she asked, "What for?"

"Being a jerk. You owed me nothing, but when you asked me to trust you, I walked away. I'm sorry for that. It took me some time to realize my anger wasn't with you at all."

"Okay," she said, remembering the moment where she could have just told him everything and things would have been so much easier. But she never blamed him for being pissed off.

"Wait, that's not where I wanted to start. I read in the papers that your father was cleared, so that's great. And they found the people who'd framed him."

"It was. I had nothing to do with it. It was all Neil. Of course he knew the right people." She inhaled. "And what you… It took me too long to realize what you'd done by having me take that picture of you and Holstrom in front of the Degas. It helped Neil convince the authorities to act. Without implicating me." She smiled self-consciously. "But of course you knew that, so thank you."

"Technically, only my arm made it into the photo."

"Neil told me you offered to testify if necessary."

Logan shrugged, modest to the end. "Have you seen your dad yet?"

She shook her head. "I can't decide whether I want to or not. I mean, I'm glad he isn't behind bars."

"You'll figure it out. Just go with your instincts."

"Yes, because it worked so well for me in Boston."

He smiled. "Actually, it did."

"You're joking, right?"

"Now, you might've had a better *plan*," he said, his lips twitching. "But you've got guts. No denying that. And you can think fast on your feet. How many people do you imagine have gotten that close to Holstrom?"

Just hearing his name made her shudder. "I only succeeded because of Neil and Sam, and most of all, you."

Logan sighed. "I didn't do you any favors by being a jerk." He looked tired. "I've been figuring some stuff out, too. Some day, I'd like to tell you about why I left the military. But right now, all I want to do is kiss you."

She was on him, literally on him, straddling his thighs, her dress riding up to her panties. All she cared about was that when their lips met, it felt better than any dream.

He put his arms around her and even though this wasn't a first kiss, it felt like one. The secrets between them had vanished, leaving the getting to know each other part for tonight and hopefully a thousand tomorrows.

"God, I've missed you," he murmured. They were both breathless. "I hope you missed me, too."

With her forehead pressed to his, nodding was a little weird. "Like crazy," she said.

He kissed her again. When it started getting too heavy to breathe, she pulled back. "My bedroom is really close."

He nodded. "You'll need to move, I think."

It wasn't easy. Not just parting, but getting off him with any grace at all. Seconds later, though, they were in her room, tossing off their clothes with abandon. He didn't throw back the covers, and she didn't care.

She hadn't realized how hard he'd gotten, or how little she cared about foreplay.

"Condom?"

She nodded at her bedside drawer. Since he was now

straddling her thighs, he reached in. That he pulled out her ribbed dildo first hardly made her blush because the next thing she knew he'd opened the packet and rolled the condom on.

The first thing he did was move between her thighs. But instead of sinking all the way inside her, he said, "This isn't because your boss called me today about funding my company."

"Good to know."

"And it's not just a fling. Not for me."

"Even better," she said, her smile matching her happiness inside.

"I know it's early." He kissed her lips softly, brushed the back of his hand across her cheek. "But I want this. I want you. Whatever it takes."

"I want that, too," she whispered.

"Good," he said. "Now, if it's all right, I'd like to make love to you."

Not trusting her voice, she nodded, and lifted her hips to meet him halfway.

* * * * *

#883 HER SEXY MARINE VALENTINE
Uniformly Hot!
by Candace Havens
To get past Valentine's Day, new friends Brody Williams and
Marigold McGuire are pretending they're in love. But their
burning-hot chemistry means the Marine and the interior
designer's make-believe is quickly becoming a super-sexy reality...

#884 COMPROMISING POSITIONS
The Wrong Bed
by Kate Hoffmann
One bed. Two owners. Sam Blackstone and Amelia Sheffield
are willing to play dirty to get what they want. But at the end of
the day, will that be the bed...or each other?

#885 SWEET SEDUCTION
by Daire St. Denis
When Daisy Sinclair finds out the man she spent the night with
is her ex-husband's new lawyer, she flips. Is Jamie Forsythe
in on helping steal her family bakery? Or was their sweet
seduction the real thing?

#886 COWBOY STRONG
Wild Western Heat
by Kelli Ireland
Tyson Covington and Mackenzie Malone were rivals...with
benefits. But when Ty is forced to put his future in Kenzie's
hands, he has to do something more dangerous than loving the
enemy: he has to trust her.

———

REQUEST YOUR FREE BOOKS!
2 FREE NOVELS PLUS 2 FREE GIFTS!

HARLEQUIN®

Blaze®

red-hot reads!

YES! Please send me 2 FREE Harlequin® Blaze® novels and my 2 FREE gifts (gifts are worth about $10). After receiving them, if I don't wish to receive any more books, I can return the shipping statement marked "cancel." If I don't cancel, I will receive 4 brand-new novels every month and be billed just $4.74 per book in the U.S. or $5.21 per book in Canada. That's a savings of at least 14% off the cover price. It's quite a bargain. Shipping and handling is just 50¢ per book in the U.S. and 75¢ per book in Canada.* I understand that accepting the 2 free books and gifts places me under no obligation to buy anything. I can always return a shipment and cancel at any time. Even if I never buy another book, the two free books and gifts are mine to keep forever.

150/350 HDN GH2D

Name	(PLEASE PRINT)
Address	Apt. #
City	State/Prov.	Zip/Postal Code

Signature (if under 18, a parent or guardian must sign)

Mail to the **Reader Service:**
IN U.S.A.: P.O. Box 1867, Buffalo, NY 14240-1867
IN CANADA: P.O. Box 609, Fort Erie, Ontario L2A 5X3

Want to try two free books from another line?
Call 1-800-873-8635 or visit www.ReaderService.com.

* Terms and prices subject to change without notice. Prices do not include applicable taxes. Sales tax applicable in N.Y. Canadian residents will be charged applicable taxes. Offer not valid in Quebec. This offer is limited to one order per household. Not valid for current subscribers to Harlequin Blaze books. All orders subject to credit approval. Credit or debit balances in a customer's account(s) may be offset by any other outstanding balance owed by or to the customer. Please allow 4 to 6 weeks for delivery. Offer available while quantities last.

Your Privacy—The Reader Service is committed to protecting your privacy. Our Privacy Policy is available online at www.ReaderService.com or upon request from the Reader Service.

We make a portion of our mailing list available to reputable third parties that offer products we believe may interest you. If you prefer that we not exchange your name with third parties, or if you wish to clarify or modify your communication preferences, please visit us at www.ReaderService.com/consumerschoice or write to us at Reader Service Preference Service, P.O. Box 9062, Buffalo, NY 14240-9062. Include your complete name and address.

SPECIAL EXCERPT FROM

HARLEQUIN

Blaze

*Daisy Sinclair is determined to get over the
embarrassment of Colin Forsythe accidentally
seeing her naked...something that he didn't seem
to mind at all!*

Read on for a sneak preview of
SWEET SEDUCTION
by New York Times *bestselling author*
Daire St. Denis

"Ms. Sinclair?"

Daisy looked up at the man standing in the doorway to
her office. Yes, he was Colin Forsythe all right. His wavy
brown hair might have been a bit longer than in the picture
beside his column, but he had the same square jaw, the
same nose—though in person it was a little crooked—
and the same full lips. While he was recognizable, his
byline picture did not do him justice. In that picture he
came off as stern, albeit in a well-coiffed, intellectual sort
of way. In person? Wow. He looked anything but. His
eyes sparkled with irreverence, his lips turned up at one
side as if he was trying to keep a sinful smile in check,
and he was just...bigger. More like a professional athlete
than a distinguished foodie.

His eyebrows rose under her appraisal. "Do I pass?"

Daisy cringed. Good-looking. Big ego. No surprise.
Obviously, he was going to make this impossible for her.
But he was Colin Forsythe, and she'd been anticipating

this interview ever since taking over Nana Sin's bakery three years ago. Of course he had to show up today of all days.

"Can we pretend, for my sake, that we're meeting for the first time, right now? That you didn't just…" Daisy paused to take a deep, composing breath. "Hello, Mr. Forsythe." She walked around her desk, hand outstretched. "I'm Daisy Sinclair. Welcome to Nana Sin's."

He rubbed his jaw as if trying to massage his face into a serious expression. It didn't work. When she was close enough, he took her hand and shook it firmly. "It's Colin."

"Colin." She set her lips in a grim line and sauntered past, head held high. At the door she turned. "Shall we?"

"Shall we what?"

Daisy rolled her eyes. "Aren't you here to see the bakery?"

In one step Colin was beside her, looking down at her. Damn, the man was tall. Not fair. And what the hell was he doing, blasting her with that sinful smile of his?

"I've already seen everything." He grinned.

She groaned.

He came closer, spoke more softly. "What I'd really like is a taste."

The way he looked at her made Daisy think he wanted to taste her.

Don't miss
SWEET SEDUCTION
by Daire St. Denis,
available March 2016 wherever
Harlequin® Blaze® books and ebooks are sold.

www.Harlequin.com

Looking for more wealthy bachelors? Fear not!
Be sure to collect these sexy reads from
Harlequin® Presents and Harlequin® Desire!

A FORBIDDEN TEMPTATION
by Anne Mather

Jack Connolly isn't looking for a woman—
until he meets Grace Spencer! Trapped in a
fake relationship to safeguard her family,
Grace knows giving in to Jack would risk
everything she holds dear… But will she
surrender to the forbidden?

Available February 16, 2016

SNOWBOUND WITH THE BOSS
(Pregnant by the Boss)
by Maureen Child

When gaming tycoon Sean Ryan is
stranded with irascible, irresistible contractor
Kate Wells, the temptation to keep each other
warm proves overwhelming. Dealing with
unexpected feelings is hard enough, but what
about an unexpected pregnancy? They're
about to find out…

Available March 1, 2016